BLOCKBUSTER

BY LISA VON BIELA

Nurse Simpson gazed at Tami through the IsoStat, the clear plastic inflatable isolation pod that served as an instant individual quarantine unit. "They're all bad in this ward, but she does seem to be the worst off of the bunch. You want to change her dressings now?"

"Yeah. She's already seeped through the ones I replaced just a few hours ago."

Dr. Tomlin took some fresh self-adhering dressing pads and premoistened antibacterial cleansing cloths in his gloved hands, then slipped the items through the IsoStat's double barrier ports near Tami's arm. He laid them next to her on the bed, then gently removed the dressing from her left forearm. Both he and Nurse Simpson gasped when they saw what lay beneath.

The entire dermis had disappeared from that portion of Tami's arm, leaving exposed muscle, seeping blood, and yellow serum. Bone showed white in several places.

"Just four hours ago, she had multiple inch-wide bloody craters in the dermis, but there was dermis and no muscle had been exposed. We'll probably have to amputate to stop this, though I doubt she would survive the procedure." Dr. Tomlin wiped down the area and placed a fresh dressing on it, for what it was worth. "I've never seen it this bad. Ten years ago, they thought the original MRSA bacteria was terrible. That was like a little contact dermatitis compared to this monster."

"Do you want to re-dress her leg as long as you're on that side?"

"Yes, please bring me some more dressing material and wipes. I wanted to start with this arm, because it's where the infection started. Hopefully, it's the worst of it."

He took the materials from Nurse Simpson and inserted them through the double barrier port near Tami's lower leg. He lifted the dressing from her calf, then froze. Last time he checked, the calf had not been nearly so advanced as the arm, but now it had only the thinnest layer of dermis left before it would also break through to muscle.

For information address Crossroad Press at 141 Brayden Dr., Hertford, NC 27944
A Gordian Knot Books Production -Gordian Knot is an imprint of Crossroad Press.
www.crossroadpress.com

Crossroad Press Trade Edition

For David, with love

IN THE YEAR 2025

PROLOGUE

Tami Freeman wiped tiny beads of sweat from her forehead with the back of her hand, then frowned. Her head felt hot as a furnace—from some damned bug or pure rage, she sure couldn't tell. Didn't matter either way because she didn't have any leave time left and she needed the pay.

She disposed of the offending email with a vicious jab of her finger. Good thing the touchscreen was made of ultratough glass. That bastard boss of hers would surely dock her pay if she cracked the thing.

The email had announced yet another overly optimistic deadline to meet—or else. Ever since she'd started working at the up-and-coming social networking service, she'd been on a constant death march. One software release after another to test and deploy. Who knew if the users noticed—or even wanted— all those changes?

Maybe they should just automate software development entirely, like they'd been threatening to for years. The way they rode her and her fellow employees, they must already believe it was nothing but a cluster of hardware and software—rather than humans—that carried out their ridiculous release schedule.

The job did, however, pay the bills pretty well for an entry-level position. Good thing, because she had racked up plenty of debts since she'd left home in a final fit of justified anger. She didn't plan to go back. No how, no way. Those days of abuse by dear old Daddy were over, no matter what she had to do.

She leaned back in her standard-issue ErgoStim chair. She despised that chair. It was just another way for the company to extract more work out of everyone. The chairs provided optimal ergonomic support for long hours at the computer, but they also contained sensors. If the chair sensed its occupant wasn't paying attention, it would emit a brief electric shock, just enough to encourage renewed focus on the job. She'd been tired lately from all the overtime she'd been putting in, and so had experienced the shock feature plenty.

Tami's face and eyes burned. She scratched at her forearm, then decided to get out of her windowless cubicle and take a break. Her throat was parched, and a free can of soda on the company's dime sounded good about now.

A brief wave of dizziness hit her as she stood. She leaned against her desk for a moment and promised herself she'd start looking for another job. Soon. This one was taking too much of a toll.

Tami gritted her teeth as she entered the break room. The company kept the lighting painfully bright to discourage lengthy breaks. She reached into the well-stocked refrigerator and grabbed a cold Mountain Dew. The caffeine might give her the boost she needed.

She sat down in a hard plastic chair at one of the little round tables and popped open the Dew. She rested the chilled can against her forehead for a moment, then chugged a good slug of the stuff. Rather than soothing her throat, the Dew burned all the way down and made her eyes water.

Tami wiped her eyes, then noticed something wrong with her left forearm. A blotchy red rash extended from wrist to elbow on the underside. Tiny pinpoints of blood oozed from where she had been scratching off and on all day. *Probably allergic to my damned job.* She made a wry face and sipped some more Dew while she rested her arm on the table to let the blood dry.

"Hey, Tami. 'Sup?" Dean Wagner, her coworker from down the hall, retrieved a Pepsi from the fridge and plopped into the chair across from her.

She took another swallow, grimacing at the burning in her throat. "Did you see the latest email? I needed to get out and chill for a few minutes after reading that thing."

"Yeah. The usual shit, huh?" Dean raised the can to his lips and stopped. "What is that?"

"What's what?"

He pointed at her forearm. "That. Looks kinda nasty."

"Oh, I don't know. I just noticed it myself. It's probably from all the stress. I feel really tired, too. I'm hoping the Dew picks me up so I can get some work done."

Dean peered at her more closely. "Your face is flushed, too. You look like you're coming down with something. You should probably see a doctor about that rash." He made a brief face of disgust and took another sip of his Pepsi.

Tami gave a dismissive wave, then tucked her arm in her lap to deflect Dean's scrutiny. "No, it's just stress. I'm sure."

A tiny bead of sweat trickled from her hairline.

BREAKOUT

CHAPTER 1

The emcee stepped to the matte black podium at the center of the expansive simulated teakwood stage. He wore a formal black tux with a white shirt and tie like that of a headwaiter in a prestigious restaurant. A slender black wireless microphone followed the curve of his right jaw like a graceful, organic appendage. He waved his hands to quiet the crowd that filled the cavernous auditorium on the Denali Labs campus.

He smiled and nodded several times as he waited for silence, then said, "Ladies and gentlemen, I present to you the CEO and founder of Denali Labs, Mr. Dan Tremaine." He extended his hand stage right, then stepped away from the podium and led the audience in a round of thunderous applause.

Absently fingering his wireless microphone, Dan stood just offstage watching his intro. He smiled and waited until the applause became nearly deafening. And why shouldn't they treat him like a rock star? He'd brought his shareholders nothing but success since he founded the company a mere five years ago. The share price knew no ceiling, and, despite being a growth company, Denali Labs had paid a generous dividend every single quarter after the first year.

He might be the new kid on the block, but he'd already garnered serious respect on Wall Street. And make no mistake, the world revolved around Wall Street now. Even the façade of regulation and wrist-slapping that was the norm ten to fifteen years ago had been openly abandoned. The sky was the limit, and he who ran Wall Street could have whatever he wanted.

In its brief history, Denali Labs had produced blockbuster after blockbuster in the world of BigPharma—all still under lucrative patents. No other BigPharma firm had ever had that degree of success in so little time. Speculation abounded as to how he'd managed it, but no one had been able to unearth the secret of his success, much less emulate it.

Dan had no intention of letting momentum like that slow. No matter what it took.

Satisfied the applause had reached a suitable crescendo, he stepped out to the podium, nodded at the emcee, then stood there and basked in the adulation as the shareholders gave him a standing ovation.

It was good to be Dan Tremaine. Very good indeed.

After his presentation and another lengthy standing ovation from his grateful shareholders, Dan slipped out a door behind the stage and into a lit bay that looked much like a miniature commuter train stop for one. His personal transportation device waited there to whisk him home in a matter of moments.

When Dan founded Denali Labs, he outsourced every aspect of the operation to minimize costs while he developed his initial product line. Once the company was established and profits began to soar, he built a special campus to house all of Denali's operations, from research to manufacturing—even his own home. The design included an underground tunnel system for his personal transportation device. The sleek glass and metal unit ran on silent electromagnetic tracks at ninety miles an hour. He could travel from one end of the enormous campus to the other— alone and undisturbed by weather, traffic, or other humans— within minutes.

Now it was time to relax and reward himself for his hard work. He stepped inside the single-person unit and sat cradled in the integral padded seat within. He pressed a button on the console in front of him and leaned back for the brief ride.

Moments later he arrived in another bay, this one just beneath his home. He stepped out of the unit and into an elevator. It took him to the main floor and opened its doors without so much as a whisper of sound. Dan stepped out into his foyer, a cavernous chamber of black-veined white granite warmly lit by unseen light sources. He knew what awaited him in the living room and smiled with anticipation as he approached.

Dan stood in the arched living room doorway and took it all in. The room itself was the size of a large apartment. Its outer wall was made entirely of WindoWall, a special glass that could be made opaque when desired, totally transparent, or anything in between. The wall faced west, commanding an impressive view of the Pacific Ocean from the house's perch high up on a reinforced bluff. Right now, a magnificent sunset lit the sky with oranges and pinks. The WindoWall polarized the light and emphasized the colors.

Lounging on the thickly padded off-white leather couch were two women: one, a tall leggy blonde; the other, a lithe little brunette. Each held a half-empty glass of champagne. The blonde raised her glass. "I'm afraid we started without you." She giggled and took another sip.

A low, gleaming black lacquer coffee table stood before the couch. On it were Dan's favorite ingredients for a good party. A bottle of Krug champagne rested in a silver ice bucket, a lone empty glass by its side. A small, matching silver tray sat to the right. On it was a small mound of fluffy white powder, a tiny blade for cutting lines, and three slim disposable tubes for their inhaling pleasure. No sense in potentially spreading germs, of course.

Dan joined the women on the couch, positioning himself between them and pouring himself a glass of champagne. "Couldn't wait for me, huh?" He took a sip, savoring the crispness of the brut Krug. "Had any of this yet?" He began chopping the mound of powder into lines.

The brunette gave a sly grin. "Oh, no. We've been waiting for you." She winked at the blonde, who took another sip of her champagne and feigned ignorance.

Dan inhaled a line and passed the tray to the brunette. He tilted his head back and breathed deeply as the drug coursed through his bloodstream. A comfortable warmth, somehow both stimulating and relaxing, spread through him, quickly reaching all the way to his fingers and toes. A glowing sense of euphoria soon followed.

So much better than cocaine, this Stardust of his. All the

benefits, but none of the harmful side effects. A nice little in-house invention, just for his personal use. Maybe someday he'd operationalize it and market it. Surely it would be another blockbuster product. But for now, it was just another perk of his job. He inhaled another line of Stardust and sipped more champagne. Then he leaned back into the comfortable couch and rested an arm on each woman.

Oh yes, it was good to be Dan Tremaine.

CHAPTER 2

Phil Horton collapsed the last empty cardboard box and stacked it with its brethren just outside his office door. He returned to his desk, sank into his creaking chair, and stared into space. The weight of responsibility for Horton Drugs already felt palpable upon his shoulders. He sighed.

Why the board had chosen him over Dennis McKenzie to assume the role of CEO was beyond him. Dennis had far broader experience—especially in turning around moribund pharma companies. Hell, he'd done it more than once, and done it well. Phil, on the other hand, had spent his entire career working in the lab at Horton Drugs. He was a scientist, for God's sake, not a manager. Until now.

No, he really *did* know why he was chosen. Because of his last name. The board was determined to keep control of Horton Drugs in the family, no matter the cost. That is how it had always been since the company was founded back in 1959 by his great-grandfather, Reggie Horton. And Phil was the next blood relative in line. That was all there was to it. Nothing to do with any evidence of innate managerial talent he'd ever demonstrated.

Not that he didn't want to keep the company alive, and not just for the sake of his own paycheck. He was proud of Horton Drugs and everything it stood for. He'd do everything he could to save it. He just didn't know if he had the skills to be a CEO at all, let alone one capable of saving a company from extinction.

A knock at the door interrupted his thoughts.

And so it begins. "Come in."

Chuck Seaforth, the CFO, stepped in, his face grim as the reaper. "Hi, Phil. How's your first day going?" His attempt at a friendly smile proved a dismal failure.

"Oh, I don't know, Chuck. How about you tell *me*?"

Chuck took a seat in front of Phil's desk and cleared his throat for a bit longer than seemed necessary. He took a deep breath and began. "Well, I'd best get right to the point. You know the company's in trouble. That's no real secret and the share price reflects it. I'm here to tell you just how much trouble."

"Let's have it." Phil braced himself for the gruesome details.

"I'll email you the detailed reports this afternoon. They show several key issues at the root of the problem. Most importantly, we've been devastated by the patent cliff in recent years. Not one Horton product isn't off patent now, or about to be quite shortly. The generic drugmakers are having us for lunch because of it. What's more, we have nothing promising in the pipeline right now to even hope to stop the bleeding. Everything in the last few years has either fizzled in testing, or another company beat us to market. Naturally, this has affected cash flow, and we've had to take on debt to help cover operations and stay alive. Some of it's at decent interest rates, but the more recent debt is at much higher rates because our credit rating is slipping."

Phil covered his face with his hands as he struggled to absorb the nonstop volley of bad news. "And did you enjoy the play, Mrs. Lincoln?" he muttered under his breath.

"Excuse me?"

"Nothing. Do we have any points in our favor at all?"

Chuck hesitated as if he had to think long and hard to dig up any positive news to report, then brightened for a moment. "Well, the physical plant was paid off years ago. We own the real estate outright, too, which helps." He stared down into his lap. "On the other hand, the facility is pretty old and maintenance costs have been creeping up. But our staff is talented, hardworking, with good Midwest values, and they do have the most current testing equipment available in the lab." He looked up again and attempted a hopeful smile, but it looked more like he was having a gas pain.

Phil spread his hands on his desk, straightened up, and tried to act like a CEO, even if he didn't feel like one. He looked Chuck in the eye. "That's a pretty damned bleak report, Chuck.

What do you suggest we do about it?"

"We need a blockbuster."

"We need a blockbuster." Phil sighed. "I'll just get right on that."

After Chuck left the room, Phil stood and went to his window to try to envision just what he could possibly do to turn the company around. He gazed out at the Horton Drugs campus. He'd always found it achingly beautiful, with its acres of rolling hills, green in the summer, white with snow in the winter. Winding, tree-edged walkways connected the various red brick buildings. The place had the appearance and feel of a university campus. Soon all the trees would display the brilliant scarlets and oranges of fall, his favorite time of year.

The setting affected the employees' attitudes, too. Horton Drugs was known for its collegial atmosphere, in contrast to some of the more modern, hotshot companies with their cold, cutthroat ways. On most temperate days, you could see employees strolling the grounds together, locked in discussion. The fresh air and natural surroundings seemed to help them clear their minds and come up with new ideas.

Phil loved Horton Drugs the way it was. He hoped he could save it without destroying what made it special. But how the hell were they going to come up with a blockbuster in time to save the company?

CHAPTER 3

Tami Freeman struggled to hear the doctor's voice through pain, through drugs—and through a wall of clear plastic. She lay in a hospital bed beneath some kind of thick plastic isolation tent. An IV dripped into her vein, feeding her drugs that made her loopy, yet hardly took the edge off the constant excruciating pain that had started only a few hours after she drank her Mountain Dew in the break room yesterday.

It seemed a lifetime ago now.

Every inch of her skin itched and burned with an intensity she could never have imagined. She wanted desperately to scratch, but her wrists and ankles were somehow bound. She writhed as best she could to try to rub at the skin on her back.

A muffled voice tried to reach her. "Tami, you have to stop that. You're going to make it worse by moving around."

"I can't stand it!" Tears ran down her face, burning her skin like acid. Tami screamed in pain. "Make it stop!"

She heard more muffled voices and saw some movement at the side of her vision. Then a softening warmth crept through her veins, giving her some peace as she moved to a place away from the pain.

Dr. Tomlin sighed. "Thanks, Nurse. I hate using that high a dose, but I don't know what else to do for her. I've never seen anyone in that much severe and unrelenting pain—though I'm not sure how much longer she's going to be with us, anyway."

Nurse Simpson gazed at Tami through the IsoStat, the clear plastic inflatable isolation pod that served as an instant individual quarantine unit. "They're all bad in this ward, but she does seem to be the worst off of the bunch. You want to change her dressings now?"

"Yeah. She's already seeped through the ones I replaced just a few hours ago."

Dr. Tomlin took some fresh self-adhering dressing pads and premoistened antibacterial cleansing cloths in his gloved hands, then slipped the items through the IsoStat's double barrier ports near Tami's arm. He laid them next to her on the bed, then gently removed the dressing from her left forearm. Both he and Nurse Simpson gasped when they saw what lay beneath.

The entire dermis had disappeared from that portion of Tami's arm, leaving exposed muscle, seeping blood, and yellow serum. Bone showed white in several places.

"Just four hours ago, she had multiple inch-wide bloody craters in the dermis, but there *was* dermis and no muscle had been exposed. We'll probably have to amputate to stop this, though I doubt she would survive the procedure." Dr. Tomlin wiped down the area and placed a fresh dressing on it, for what it was worth. "I've never seen it this bad. Ten years ago, they thought the original MRSA bacteria was terrible. That was like a little contact dermatitis compared to this monster."

"Do you want to re-dress her leg as long as you're on that side?"

"Yes, please bring me some more dressing material and wipes. I wanted to start with this arm, because it's where the infection started. Hopefully, it's the worst of it."

He took the materials from Nurse Simpson and inserted them through the double barrier port near Tami's lower leg. He lifted the dressing from her calf, then froze. Last time he checked, the calf had not been nearly so advanced as the arm, but now it had only the thinnest layer of dermis left before it would also break through to muscle.

"Oh my God. This really *can't* be stopped. I can't amputate this away, and the antibiotics have done absolutely nothing. It's only a matter of time—and probably not much time—before it attacks the skin on her trunk as well. I don't know what else we can do for her except try to keep her clean and comfortable."

"The others aren't as far along in terms of tissue destruction,

but the antibiotics have been doing nothing for them, either."
Nurse Simpson turned several shades paler. "I don't even want
to think about them all degrading to this level."

Dr. Tomlin slid the used dressings through another port built
into the IsoStat. It led to a replaceable clear plastic biohazard
receptacle that would later be sealed for removal and disposal
in the burn room. Damned straight he was taking no chances
with this stuff.

"I'm afraid not only will the other patients follow suit,
but we'll see more admissions soon—and I don't know what
we're going to be able to do about it." He gazed down at Tami's
sleeping, ravaged body. "What's worse, I hear all the major cities
are seeing admissions like this. If the powers that be haven't
declared this MRSA-II outbreak an epidemic, they should soon."

CHAPTER 4

"I can't believe we finally did it." Sylvia Creston reached across the restaurant table and squeezed her new husband's hand. "But I'm glad we did."

Todd Barrett laughed. "Some people just take longer to get to things, I suppose." His expression turned serious. "I don't know if I would have done anything differently, though. I'm glad we took the time to establish ourselves—you in your research work and me teaching at the law school now. Our lives are on course, so there are fewer distractions for us. I almost wonder if it isn't harder to commit earlier when there are so many things competing for attention."

"I hadn't thought of it that way, but you have a point. All I know is, it feels right for us, and that's all that matters." Sylvia raised her glass of chardonnay in a toast. "To us."

"To us." Todd clicked his glass to hers, then gazed out the window at the orange and pink sunset tinting the Oregon coast. "Look at that amazing view. I'm glad we came here. We have the lodge for dinner and the little cabin for privacy—and the ocean, too. Doesn't get much better than that."

Sylvia set down her glass and fussed with the last bits of rice on her dinner plate. "I already know I'm going to hate packing up and leaving tomorrow. What a perfect place for our honeymoon."

"Yeah, I'm going to miss our walks on the beach. None of that back home in the Midwest." He sighed. "It's nearly fall, and fall just never lasts long enough before winter."

Sylvia feigned a shiver and smiled. "Don't remind me."

"Soon I'll face a whole new crop of 1Ls. I wonder what this class will be like. Sometimes you get a couple of astoundingly brilliant students; sometimes not. They all seem to share that deer-in-the-headlights look for the first couple of weeks anyway." He chuckled. "Some of them are a little too terrified for their own good. I had one a couple years ago, first time I cold-called her she got really, really pale, then passed right out."

"Oh no, you're kidding!"

"Nope. Down she went. I hope she chilled out some by the time she graduated, or she'll be the subject of one of those epic bar exam stories where someone throws up or has some sort of meltdown right during the test."

Seized with a hilarious mental image, Sylvia clamped her hand over her mouth to stifle herself. The atmosphere in the lodge's dining room wasn't snooty, but hysterical laughter probably wouldn't be appreciated by their fellow patrons.

"There are some good stories to be told. I should write a book someday." Todd took another sip of his wine.

"Sounds like it. Things are a little more staid where I work." Sylvia gazed out the window before continuing. "But, there may be some drama soon. The new CEO should have started this week. Our market share has been slipping—badly—and I wonder what he'll do to turn the boat around."

"Are you worried for your job?"

"Not yet, but ..." Sylvia sipped the last of her wine. "You know, let's not talk about work yet, okay? Let's have a nice walk by the ocean while we still can." She smiled. "And then we can warm up in the cabin next to the fireplace. What do you think about that?"

"I think that's a fine idea." Todd shot her a knowing glance and signaled for the check.

CHAPTER 5

President Andrew Coleridge did not like what he was seeing, but, like any good train wreck, the news was impossible to ignore.

Flat-panel monitors covered one entire wall of the Oval Office. Normally, each ran a different feed: the stock market, world news, U.S. news, world weather, natural disasters, and more. Without leaving his desk, the president could keep up on everything of importance. He found the monitor arrangement easier on his older eyes than the smaller virtual displays that were the latest technology. He had too much to track to try to do it on such a small platform, despite the ultrahigh resolution offered by the latest generation.

Today, one topic dominated the news so completely that all the monitors covered the same story from one or another perspective.

All eyes were on MRSA-II, the apparent successor to the so-called "flesh eating" bacteria from about ten years back, the ominous Methicillin-Resistant Staphylococcus Aureus. Only MRSA-II took the etiology to grave new heights. It spread among its victims with frightening ease, moved much more rapidly through the body, ate flesh clear down to the bone in a matter of days and sometimes hours in weaker souls, and was so fast-moving that even early amputation couldn't stop it.

The damned thing was filling hospitals' isolation wards to capacity, and all staff were stretched to their limits trying to stem the tide. No drug currently available slowed it in the slightest.

At this point, there were no known survivors.

President Coleridge couldn't help but wonder if MRSA-II had been deliberately designed and turned loose in the Homeland by some America-hating bioterrorist. That was, after all, the doomsday scenario every sitting president in the modern era had to grapple with. No matter how carefully the government tried to control access, the means and materials were within the reach of armchair terrorists, and had been for some time. Hell, his predecessor had nearly gone ahead and done just this, but against a Third World nation that had fallen from favor and into the arms of a known enemy country.

But regardless of its source, it was here, and it was wreaking havoc *now*. The stock market was nearly in free fall, and people were afraid to go to work or to go shopping, so the economy was beginning a deadly downward spiral. The disease hadn't yet spread beyond the borders of the Homeland, but surely it was only a matter of time before it did—and when it did, the consequences would be grave. This had to be fixed, and quickly.

An expected knock sounded on his door. "Come in."

John Humphrey, his secretary of Health and Human Services, stepped in and took a seat. His haggard face betrayed the sleepless nights he'd spent tracking the outbreak over the last several weeks. "Good morning, Mr. President."

"Nothing good about it that I can see. What do you have?"

Humphrey let out a weary breath. "Well, between you and me, this passed from outbreak to full-blown epidemic several weeks ago." He looked the president in the eye. "But you know as well as I do, if we put that label on it, there will be panic in the streets—worse than there is already. I don't dare use the word, but yes sir, this is an epidemic."

"What can be done?"

Humphrey ran a hand through his hair and stared at his shoes. "Damned thing's resistant to every antibiotic ever made. Nothing stops it. Nothing topical, nothing systemic. It leaps from victim to victim and consumes. It's exponentially more vicious than the original MRSA. Given how it's so readily transmissible before a person even knows they're sick, even strict quarantine measures offer a pretty weak defense."

President Coleridge slammed his fist on his desk. "So we're

in a national emergency, and we're at fucking square one, is that it?"

Humphrey flinched visibly. "I wish I could tell you otherwise."

"All right, thanks. You can go now. I need to think." He waved his secretary away.

John Humphrey raised himself up from his chair as if he were forty years older than he was, and left without another word.

Alone in the Oval Office, President Coleridge turned away from the wall of flat-panel displays and stared out the window onto the White House lawn. He had to think big and he had to think fast. None of his cabinet seemed to have any bright ideas and the death toll was mounting.

After an hour or so of weighing different ideas and discarding them just as quickly, it hit him.

President Coleridge made the needed calls to set his plan in motion.

CHAPTER 6

Dan Tremaine loosened his seat belt and relaxed in the charcoal gray leather airplane seat. At least his corporate jet provided all his preferred amenities. The trip would be short, comfortable, and possibly quite useful. But still, he couldn't decide whether to be annoyed or delighted. On the one hand, he had other things to do, and resented being summoned—yes, summoned—to a meeting with the President.

But, on the other hand, this meeting confirmed the value of Denali Labs' massive donations to President Coleridge. Over time, the favor those dollars bought had resulted in much more BigPharma-friendly laws, as well as the political castration of the FDA. Back in the day, the FDA actually had funding and some regulatory teeth. But now, staffing had been cut so severely that new drugs were approved by rubber stamp, resulting in quite a monetary savings for companies like Denali Labs. Even better, you could pay a modest fee to have your drug fast-tracked.

All of this made bringing a new drug to market a snap, compared to the expensive process that had been the norm a mere decade ago. Dan took full advantage of the weak regulatory environment to implement his proprietary business plan—and the combination worked. Denali Labs shocked the industry when it went from startup to market leader in an unprecedented amount of time.

Dan gazed at the meticulously prepared selection on the rectangular black plate before him. He chose a piece of fresh tuna sashimi and popped it into his mouth. He savored the morsel, then took a sip of warm sake as he pondered the situation.

President Coleridge had personally called him yesterday to

request his presence later today. He'd only said that the matter was urgent; he'd provided no clue whatever concerning the subject of the meeting. Dan liked to be prepared and in control of every situation, and this made him uneasy.

Dan nudged his left shirt cuff to reveal his PortiComm, the popular watch-like apparatus that provided ubiquitous Internet connectivity, access to files in the cloud, and voice communications. He pressed a small button on its side, then rested his left forearm on the table and waited for a moment. The FloaTouch screen, an illuminated horizontal area of roughly one foot by two feet, appeared in the air at eye level. When he touched it with the palm of his right hand, a series of colored tiles appeared along the edges of the glowing rectangle. He touched one of the tiles with his right index finger and a news site appeared in the center. He scrolled through the stories to quickly update himself.

... New version of the popular personal robot, CyborgPal, set for release in a week, and rumored to have software bugs...

... Several deaths reported at a commune established by those who still believe global warming is a farce; deaths caused by massive heat wave ...

... FDA and USDA both deem GMO beef safe for human consumption; stock price for BetterBeef soars on the news ...

... MRSA-II outbreak continues to spread, still no known cure; CDC advises staying home as much as possible ...

Dan Tremaine smiled.

Phil Horton fidgeted in his cramped coach seat. His predecessor sold off the Horton Drugs corporate jet last year in a fit of austerity. Phil knew it was just one of many expenses that had to be cut to keep the company alive this long, but now he wished he still had it, if only for this trip.

He hated flying at all, let alone commercially—and to him, flying coach presented just one more layer of horror to knock him off his stride. The last thing he needed was all this inconvenience and annoyance, when he desperately needed to collect himself, focus and prepare.

But prepare for what? While, like every major corporation, Horton Drugs had contributed to President Coleridge's coffers over the years, he'd never met the man. Hell, he'd never even spoken to him until that odd call yesterday demanding his presence today. He had no idea what Coleridge wanted, so he hadn't the slightest clue what he should be doing to prepare. He'd only taken over the Horton Drugs reins days ago, and didn't even have a grip on his new position. And now he had to drop everything and head for Washington? It just didn't make sense. But you just don't say *no* to the president.

He sighed as he gazed at the turn-of-the-century equipment the airline provided its coach passengers. The five-inch-square hardware-based monitor in the seat-back in front of him looked like something from another world. But it was all he had while stuck on this flight from hell. He slid the cheap headset over his ears, powered on the monitor, and selected a newsfeed to view. Then he decided he didn't want to be agitated by the news of the day, and changed the channel to MindRelease.

White noise played in the headset while shapes and colors with no apparent pattern moved across the screen. MindRelease videos supposedly presented relaxing subliminal messages. He hoped that was all. Phil generally distrusted what he couldn't see and confirm with his own eyes, but today he needed something to help calm him ahead of his meeting with the president. He didn't want to risk taking a drug that could linger and dull him later.

He leaned back in the stiff seat, rolled his shoulders to try to loosen them, and then gave over his attention to the sounds in his ears and the images on the screen. After a while, he found he was able to detach himself from his uncomfortable surroundings and relax. A little.

CHAPTER 7

D r. Tomlin took a deep breath to brace himself and stepped out of the doctors' lounge to face the day. Out in the hall, he encountered Nurse Simpson.

She peered at him, then scowled. "You look terrible. When did you last sleep?"

Dr. Tomlin had to think before he could answer—not a good sign. "Oh, I think I caught a catnap yesterday. Lucky to get that."

The isolation ward was filled to capacity—and then some. A couple dozen of the more recent arrivals were stacked in the hallway, each beneath an individual IsoStat. At least they still had plenty of those in the supply room. All staff doctors had been called in for indefinite duty, and every one of them was as tired and haggard as he was.

Now it was time for morning rounds, starting with the most critical cases. And that meant Tami Freeman, the first of the wave to arrive several days ago. She'd been going downhill fast despite their best efforts, and he feared what he would find when he looked in on her.

He nodded at Nurse Simpson. "Ready to start rounds?"

"Ready as a person *can* be, under the circumstances." She attempted to smile, but her lips only formed a grim line.

They walked in silence down the harshly lit hall until they reached the main isolation ward. A double-doored vestibule controlled access to the ward to prevent contamination of the rest of the hospital. Dr. Tomlin opened the vestibule's outer door and they stepped inside. Shelves of disposable sterile garb lined the left and right walls. The inner door to the actual ward opened from the opposite wall. A bin for used items stood next to it.

As they donned their protective sterile booties, gowns, caps, masks, and gloves, Dr. Tomlin reflected on how much his routine had changed in just the last week. They usually had a few patients in the isolation ward with some contagious disease or another. Now, there were so many, it felt as if the rest of the hospital had faded into oblivion. Were any babies being delivered these days? What about good old-fashioned broken bones, strokes, and heart attacks? It almost felt like there was no other reality except the overflowing isolation ward.

Dr. Tomlin rested his hand on the door handle. "Ready?"

Nurse Simpson nodded as she made a final adjustment to her mask.

They walked past the other patients in their IsoStats and went straight to Tami's bed. Despite himself, Dr. Tomlin had hoped she would show some sign—*any* sign—of improvement. His heart sank when he looked at her.

She displayed evident and severe distress, worse than ever. Her mouth gaped in obvious hypoxia, despite the stream of oxygen being pumped into her IsoStat. The blue of impending death tinged her skin—what there was of it.

Dr. Tomlin leaned over and looked at her more closely through the clear plastic. Her lesions had progressed to the point where there was no use in trying to dress them individually, or else Tami would have been in one solid dressing from head to toe. Even if it were possible to keep up with the lesions' spread, it would generate vast quantities of biohazard material to dispose of. There was already a backup of materials for disposal in the burn room in the hospital's basement. No sense in adding to it without good reason.

So there she lay, covered in a thin hospital gown seeped through with blood and serum, her limbs nothing more than bloody pulp with the bone showing here and there. The IV that brought her nourishment and replacement fluids had been relocated to a much deeper blood vessel near her clavicle, as the usual arm veins were now exposed and in danger of eroding entirely from the ravages of the bacteria.

Tami's pain had become so severe, Dr. Tomlin had placed her in a medically induced coma. He'd never seen anyone in that much pain, and he'd been helpless to alleviate it any other way. No pain med, no matter how strong, had even come close to bringing her the slightest relief.

Unfortunately, she'd been in too much distress to give them any family member names before being placed in the coma, and she hadn't carried any useful information in her purse. So they'd been unable to notify anyone of her condition.

As difficult as it was to watch Tami struggle and falter, Dr. Tomlin knew this was only the beginning of a terrible tsunami. She'd been the first patient, and the ones who followed her were more than likely going to take this very same path unless they found a drug to combat this vicious bacteria—and fast. His shoulders slumped as he considered the implications for those jamming the ward now, and for those who would surely be arriving in the coming days.

"Doctor, look!" Nurse Simpson pointed to a quickly spreading pool of fresh blood at thigh level on Tami's gown.

Jarred out of his dismal reverie, Dr. Tomlin thrust his gloved hands through the double barrier port closest to the bleeding. He pulled up Tami's gown to reveal the source of the blood, then groaned. The bacteria that had been decimating the tissues of her limbs now had eaten right through the femoral artery. If he didn't act quickly, Tami would soon bleed out.

But what could he do? Amputate? Cauterize? *All* her veins and arteries were in danger of this very thing as the hideous MRSA-II bacteria ate her alive. There wasn't enough solid tissue there to patch or stitch or cauterize. There just wasn't.

So he did the only thing he could do for her. He held Tami's hand for the few brief moments it took for what was left of her blood to drain from her body. The arterial flow became weaker and weaker as her heart gave up the fight.

Nurse Simpson and Dr. Tomlin shared a quiet moment with bowed heads, then he said, "Have the body incinerated along with all the biohazard waste. Destroy it all."

Dr. Tomlin straightened up and clenched his jaw. Without another word, he stepped over to the next patient to see what, if anything, he could do.

CHAPTER 8

President Coleridge pressed a button at the side of his desk. All the flat-panel monitors went black simultaneously. He didn't want any distractions during this meeting. He had to set the right tone—and he had to get results. Nothing else was an option.

He mentally reviewed his proposal as he sat back in his chair and waited for his guests to arrive. He'd made his choices with care. Denali Labs was top dog in BigPharma right now. They seemed to have the Midas touch, and might very well be able to deliver something fast.

Horton Drugs, on the other hand, was more of a long shot. In prior years, they'd been the ones to beat. Their performance since the company's inception had been solid, stable—predictably good. But, for whatever reason, their ability to innovate seemed to have fallen by the wayside in recent years. Combine that with the on-fire performance of Denali, and Horton had been left behind like yesterday's news.

That meant they'd be hungry. They needed a blockbuster now, or they'd likely disappear from the map within another year or so, depending on what financial reserves they still had left from better times.

He'd deliberated whether he should enlist more participants to ensure success. But the fewer who knew about this plan, the better. Hopefully, his judgment had been sound. The security— even the survival—of the Homeland depended on it.

A knock at the door interrupted his thoughts. "Send them in." He was anxious to get this plan moving.

In stepped Dan Tremaine and Phil Horton. He knew them

both from their publicity photos, but even if he hadn't, he could have easily guessed which was which.

Dan Tremaine stood erect and exhibited a somewhat haughty demeanor. He had an intelligent, almost conniving, look in his eye. Coleridge found his appearance irritating in its lack of deference, yet encouraging at the same time, given the stakes and the nature of his plan.

Phil Horton, on the other hand, looked intimidated, almost lost. He looked like he wanted to shrink into the wallpaper as he cast furtive glances around the room. He gave the impression of someone incapable of bold, assertive action. Coleridge hoped he had more to bring to the table than it appeared.

"Sit down, please. Let's get right to it." He steepled his fingers and waited as they both settled into their chairs and gave him their attention. "First, I don't want any of this leaked to the press. You'll understand why momentarily. You will share the minimum information necessary internally within your companies, but that's all. I'm sure you're both well aware of the MRSA-II outbreak, and the gravity of the situation. A cure must be found. That's why you're here."

Tremaine sat back and crossed his leg over his knee. Horton sat up straight, his eyes wide. His hands fidgeted on the arms of his chair.

"We don't have time for the usual market forces to act for BigPharma to find the cure, so I've selected you both for a competition. Whichever of your firms develops the cure for MRSA-II first will receive an exclusive, *lucrative*, government contract for the drug, and would retain the patent rights. I want to purchase the drug in volume and arrange for an optimized, fast-track rollout. Fees for FDA approval would be waived, and the federal government would bear all manufacturing and distribution costs. You can see why I don't want this all over the news. If the public got wind that the government was this concerned, well, the panic would spiral out of control. Commerce and the markets are already taking huge hits."

Horton found his voice. Barely. "Why us, Mr. President?"

"I need concentrated effort, and I don't want to multiply the potential for leaks. Horton Drugs has a reputation for good products, but, well, not so much lately. You may be due for an important breakthrough, and the Homeland needs it now." He nodded toward Tremaine. "And Denali's been on a roll. I'm hedging my bets."

He stood to signal the end of the meeting. "I trust I've made myself clear. Good luck to both of you. Let me know as soon as you have something. I'll be sure you each receive cultures of the MRSA-II bacteria to get started with."

CHAPTER 9

Back in his office the next day, Phil Horton planned his response to the president's challenge. He anticipated no problem keeping it under wraps. Horton Drugs didn't have much to crow about these days, and he was happy to stay in the shadows until he was able to turn the company around—or not.

But could they do it? That was the tougher question. They were head-to-head with only one other competitor. Unfortunately, Denali was one hell of a competitor to be up against. But if they succeeded, this *could* save the company. He had to give it the best shot possible.

He would put his two best drug developers on it. Jerry Bennigan had been with Horton Drugs for nearly twenty-five years. He knew the ropes, and he'd been responsible for several major drug breakthroughs over the years. Just not lately. Sylvia Creston was newer, had been with the company maybe three years. She was younger, and trained in more modern techniques. Just back from her honeymoon, she should be rested and ready to tackle something new. Together, they should make a good pair for the project.

Phil checked the time on the PortiComm on his left wrist. They were due to arrive in his office momentarily. He'd pulled the same trick as had the president, in scheduling a critical meeting and providing no advance information about the subject matter. He figured he'd better warn them about the secrecy of the project before he told them any details. That should keep the risk of leakage down from the get-go.

Moments later, they arrived at his open door. He motioned to them. "Come in, sit down."

They both took their seats, each wearing a worried look. It occurred to Phil that, given even the public information concerning the state of the company's finances, they might be expecting their pink slips. Jerry had a lot of seniority at stake, and Sylvia had just gotten married. He couldn't blame them for being nervous, and his secrecy had undoubtedly compounded their anxiety, so he got right to business.

"I have a new project for both of you. It's critically important." The worried looks eased somewhat. "First, I have to impress on you that this is highly confidential and word of it must not go outside the company."

They glanced at each other, then both nodded in agreement.

"Good. Well, I'm sure you're aware of the severity of the MRSA-II outbreak. I want you to find the cure, and I need you to do it as quickly as possible. The sample culture should arrive today, if it hasn't already."

"Who's sending the sample? Is someone sponsoring the work?" Jerry leaned forward in his chair, looking eager to get started.

Phil briefly debated how much to tell them. The president had been adamant about secrecy, and the more he revealed, the greater the chance for a leak—whether accidental or on purpose. It would be truthful enough just to say this was an all-out effort to save the company—and conquer a terrible disease at the same time. He hesitated a moment more while he looked into their eyes. They deserved the truth.

"This stays among us. The president called Dan Tremaine and me to the White House yesterday."

Sylvia sat upright with a startled look on her face, and Jerry muttered, "Wow."

Phil continued. "He put us in a direct—and very secret— competition with Denali Labs to come up with the cure. Whoever wins gets a massive government contract for the drug. So massive, that if we get there first, we save Horton Drugs for sure. If they get there first, I figure we're probably looking at the end of the road. You're the best I have. Good luck, for all our sakes."

"We'll do our very best," said Sylvia as she and Jerry stood to leave.

"Thanks."

Once they were gone, Phil went over and closed his office door. Then he sat down at his desk, strangely exhausted from the brief meeting. He knew Horton was in serious trouble, but somehow uttering the words aloud to two of his staff made the dismal fact seem far more real.

He rested his face in his hands. They just *had* to find the cure first.

CHAPTER 10

Still struggling to grasp what Phil had just told them, Jerry walked down the hall with Sylvia. He stopped and motioned toward an empty meeting room on their right. "Can we talk for a minute? Somehow, I'm not quite ready to head straight for the lab without thinking this through a little first."

"Sure. I know what you mean. I'm still blown away myself."

As they stepped inside, the room lights automatically came on, revealing unadorned white walls and a glass meeting table that could accommodate six. Jerry shut the door, then sat across the table from Sylvia. They both stared down at the table and, for a moment, neither spoke.

Jerry blew out a breath and started. "Well, I never thought I'd have an assignment like this. The president. And a secret competition. Unreal."

"No kidding. He must be really concerned about the outbreak to do something like this. That can only mean the media must be downplaying the story."

"If that's true, it must be *really* bad out there. I'd say we have our work cut out for us to tackle something like this. All I know about that pathogen right now is what I've gathered from the news reports." He shrugged. "Feels like we're starting a race off our back foot."

"Well, it's incredibly vicious. I know that much. We'll need to employ the maximum security protocol to make sure it's kept contained while we work on it. Frankly, it makes me a little nervous to work with it at all, but I suppose someone has to do it."

"I've studied a lot of pathogens over the years, but nothing quite like this one. We should review the security protocol and make damned sure it's sufficient before we get started. We can't risk exposure."

"Agreed. I wouldn't mind taking extra precautions on this one."

"Of course, if we fail to find a cure, this could very well be our final project anyway. I think this is the last gasp for Horton Drugs."

Sylvia lowered her eyes and spoke in a soft voice. "Yeah. Seems like tough enough odds to start with, but competing against Denali, of all things. They've been unbeatable in the marketplace lately." She sighed.

Jerry looked away as he spoke. He didn't want to reveal the true depth of his feelings for Horton Drugs. By his standards, that would be unprofessional. Just as unprofessional as revealing how he felt about Sylvia, now a married woman. "You know, I've been here a long time and things have sure changed a lot in that time. I was here back when Horton was the high flyer and there were more barriers to upstarts like Denali just suddenly appearing on the scene. Back when FDA approval had some teeth. Back when we had to run human trials before a drug could be approved."

"I can't imagine having to test that way—with human trials, that is. Seems so barbaric. I remember reading about protests back in the day about using monkeys and other lab animals. Amazing scientists had to work that way then."

He faced Sylvia again, and tried hard to conceal his attraction to her by following her lead in the conversation. "You've never had to conduct one, have you? I keep forgetting that. Well, it's one thing about the good old days I don't miss. Had a lot of sleepless nights when we were in a human trial. You could run the old-style bench trials from here to eternity and still not know what a drug would do in an actual human body. There was always the chance of something surprising coming up, some crazy interaction. You couldn't skip the human trial phase for that reason, but my God it was frightening waiting to see if something terrible happened."

"That's awful. I'm glad I came into the profession when technology replaced that sort of thing—or I probably never would have entered the field."

"We're going to need all the advantages current technology offers, that's for sure. We'll need fast and accurate test cycles. But we'll still need some luck to find a promising direction early enough to beat out Denali."

"We're the best Horton has, right? So if anyone here can do it, it's us." Sylvia smiled. "Seriously, I know you've spent your entire career with Horton, and I've only been here a few years. But I like it here and I want to see the place survive, too. I don't like the cowboy mentality at places like Denali. So, let's put our heads together and do this." She offered her hand.

Jerry shook her hand and smiled, relieved that she was at least as committed as he was, despite the odds. "Deal."

He released her hand quickly before he could succumb to the temptation to let the touch linger and possibly alert her to his feelings. He'd never worked directly with her until now, but he'd noticed her beauty and intelligence in staff meetings ever since she'd started at Horton. He'd never dared approach her, given their age difference, and now that she was newly married, it was too late.

Whether they won or lost the competition in the end, he already knew working with Sylvia on this project would bring him the pleasure of her nearness—along with the agony of knowing she could never be his, no matter how much he wanted her.

CHAPTER 11

Vince Calhoun knocked on Dan Tremaine's office door at the scheduled time. Ever the one for suspense and drama, Dan hadn't told him what the meeting was about. Vince hoped it concerned the MRSA-II outbreak. He'd been watching the news, and things were getting dire. Too dire. Dan had waited entirely too long.

This bug was far more dangerous than any other of its kind, and—though the media had not yet uttered the word—Vince believed the outbreak had reached the scale of a full-blown epidemic. He hoped it wasn't too late to act, that the pathogen could still be contained.

"Come in."

Vince stepped inside and took a seat. As usual, he hid his disgust at the sight of Dan's ostentatious office. He preferred bare-boned practicality to adornment, so much so that his own office featured no personal effects at all, and certainly no clutter. Dan's office, on the other hand, screamed self-importance. Plaques, photos with celebrities and politicians, and tasteless artwork-du-jour that looked like the product of drunken monkeys took up every bit of wall space. Gaudy little trinkets littered Dan's desktop. Vince valued the work of Denali Labs for the innovative products it produced, and felt such egomania served no useful purpose. At least in his opinion.

Despite their divergent personalities, the two had forged a solid working relationship. Dan valued Vince's consistently groundbreaking work and so viewed him as a sort of right-hand man and compensated him accordingly. Consequently, Vince spent a lot of time enduring the sight of Dan's office in frequent strategy sessions.

"So, what did you want to see me about?"

Dan beamed. "You won't believe where I was yesterday."

"Where?"

"Met with President Coleridge."

Vince raised an eyebrow. "Oh?"

"Yes. He's concerned about the MRSA-II problem, and had a proposition to make."

"He *should* be concerned. What's the proposition?"

Dan told Vince the details of his meeting with Phil Horton and the president. "So it just comes down to the matter of timing."

"Why not right away?"

"No, I don't like the way that would look. Besides, if this goes on a little longer, it's all the better publicity—and demand."

Vince leaned forward in his chair and looked Dan squarely in the eye. "This is a dangerous game you're playing. From what I've seen, the cure can't get out there fast enough. People are dying. Lots of them. It'll get a whole lot worse out there—and fast—given the contagion profile."

Dan waved a dismissive hand. "Sometimes you're too conservative, Vince. We'll wait. Not a long time, but a little more."

"But—"

Dan cast him a glare. "Don't argue with me on this. I'll let you know when it's time." He softened his tone. "Oh, and could you make up another batch of Stardust in the next couple of days? Got a party coming up and I'm getting a little low."

"Sure."

Vince clamped his mouth shut, then quickly stood and exited the room before he could say something he'd regret. He closed the door behind him and paused just outside Dan's office for a moment as he tried to collect himself.

Dan had made a spectacular success of Denali Labs, true enough. He knew venture capital and schmoozing, but he couldn't operate lab equipment or analyze the genome of a bacteria if his life depended on it. No, Dan couldn't have established Denali as he had without Vince's skills and experience, and he knew it. Despite that, he sometimes seemed to forget those details and treated Vince like some lackey.

Like that damned Stardust. One day Dan had asked him if he could develop a cocaine-like drug in the lab. He did it, just to see if he could, and regretted it ever since. Dan tried the stuff, liked it, and had started using it routinely, not just for parties. It seemed to inflate his ego even more when he'd had a few snorts. And ever since, he'd periodically asked Vince to replenish his supply, like some personal pharmacist.

Vince took several deep breaths to calm himself as he realized his hands were shaking and he had his teeth clenched so tightly he risked cracking a tooth. He headed back to the refuge of his office for the time being.

He hoped Dan would soon see the light and allow him to prepare the MRSA-II cure for release.

CHAPTER 12

Tired and anxious to put the work day behind her, Sylvia pulled into the garage and switched off her electromag-powered car. To her relief, Todd's car wasn't yet there, so he must be running late, too. She needed a little time to herself to sort out what had transpired that day—and how she was going to handle it at home, given the confidential nature of her new project.

She went inside and dropped her bag on a kitchen chair. Then she headed upstairs to change out of her work clothes and into her favorite sweats and T-shirt. She dressed casually for work, but always changed as soon as she arrived home, just on the off chance there was any contamination. She observed proper lab protocol religiously, so she knew this ritual was just a little compulsive fixation on her part.

Barefoot and feeling a little more relaxed already, she returned to the kitchen. She took a wineglass from the cupboard and poured herself some chilled chardonnay. Todd hadn't texted her that he would be late, so she assumed he would arrive home shortly.

Sylvia pressed a button on the refrigerator's side panel. The door's molecules dutifully changed state to allow her to see inside without opening the door and wasting energy. Unable to decide what to make for dinner, she sat down at the kitchen table with her wine and sipped a little while she stared and waited for inspiration.

The chilling implications of the earlier conversation with Phil distracted her from planning dinner. If the media was holding anything back about the outbreak, then just how bad *was* it out there?

And of course, the future of Horton Drugs lay on her and Jerry's shoulders. No pressure there.

The secrecy surrounding the project disturbed her, too. She'd known Todd for years. They'd never kept things from each other, and they'd only just gotten married. Seemed like a bad way to start off their marriage, keeping an important aspect of her work from him. But if she told him, she might put him in a terrible situation. He was, after all, a lawyer. A lawyer who happened to teach ethics, among other subjects. If she did let him in on it, swearing him in turn to secrecy, that could create a problem for him.

Bells cannot be unrung, though. Maybe best to keep quiet about it at home, at least for now, until she knew more and could better gauge the situation from all angles.

She sighed, stood, and stared once more through the fridge's transparent door. Inspiration still eluded her, but there were salad fixings. That was a start. There were steaks in the freezer, too. She pressed the button again to return the door to its normal opaque black gleam, then opened it and reached inside for the needed items. She unwrapped the steaks, put them in the ZapperBox, and pressed a button to instantly thaw them.

Her ruminations caused Sylvia to lose track of her surroundings. She nearly dropped the lettuce when she heard the garage door opening for Todd. Determined to act normal, she started washing the salad vegetables as though she weren't the keeper of state secrets.

"Hey, how long have you been home?" Todd strode in with a smile, put his arms around her, and gave her a lingering kiss on the lips.

"Well, hello to you, too." She smiled. "I haven't been home that long. Figured I'd get started on dinner."

"Sounds good. I didn't have time for lunch today. Had a bunch of confused 1Ls storm the office with questions. By the time they cleared out, it was time for my next class. Next thing you know, the day got away from me entirely."

"I know how that can happen."

"So, how was your day?"

Sylvia struggled to decide just how much to say, and settled on what she hoped was a safe enough compromise. "Oh, fine. Got a new assignment today. Phil wants us to try to find a drug to combat that MRSA-II that's been going around."

Todd cracked open a beer and shot her a concerned look. "Really? I've seen the news reports on that. It sounds exceptionally nasty. Be careful working with it, okay?"

"I will. Don't worry. We have protocols for handling pathogens to avoid exposure. I plan to review them before I get started, and maybe take more precautions than they require—if that's even possible."

"All right. You know, I have an early lecture tomorrow that I need to prepare a few notes for. If you don't mind, I'd like to get that out of the way while you're making dinner, then I can relax the rest of the evening."

"Sure, no problem."

Sylvia took a deep, relieved breath after Todd left the kitchen. Her story seemed to have satisfied him without revealing too much. She turned on her range top's indoor flame grill and retrieved the thawed steaks from the ZapperBox.

She'd tell Todd the whole story when the project wrapped up. Meanwhile, she'd make them a nice dinner and quit worrying. At least for now.

CHAPTER 13

"Doctor, you look like you're about to collapse. Here, sit down for a minute and let me get you some water."

"Huh? Oh, yeah, okay, I guess I should sit for a minute." Dr. Miller flopped down into a nearby plastic chair in a corner of the small hospital ward. He hadn't felt this weak and tired in years, not since his residency so many years ago.

"Here you go." The nurse handed him a paper cup of cool water.

He gratefully accepted it and took a long drink before speaking again. "Thank you so much. I'm really beat. I'm just an old country doctor out in the sticks. Never expected to have to deal with some big city epidemic." He rubbed his burning eyes with the back of his gowned arm. "My God, I've got no backup staff, no meds, nothing to fight this with. I never dreamed something like this would get all the way out here."

The nurse sat in a chair next to him, leaned over, and massaged her tired calves as she spoke. "I know. I can't believe it made it out here, either. And not just one patient, but a half dozen already. I'm scared how many more we can take on if this gets worse."

"I honestly don't know *what* we're going to do." He waved a hand in the general direction of the line of beds in the ward. "These people should be in strict quarantine, and we just don't have the facilities for it. I'm going to have to call the hospital in the next town over and see if they can take some of them. I'm afraid, though, that they've already exposed others anyway, and so there'll be more to come."

"And nothing seems to work. Mr. Jones on the end there

looks like he's just about run out of fight. He's elderly to start with, and that *thing* has eaten almost through his skin on both his arms."

"I know." Dr. Miller stared at the floor. "I don't think he'll be with us much longer. He was frail to begin with—I'd just given him his annual exam." He pointed to the surgical mask covering his face. "I don't think this is enough to shield us from this one. I've been changing gloves and dumping dressings and such in the burn barrel, but I somehow doubt it will be enough against this bug."

The nurse looked away, a tear forming in her eye.

She remained silent.

Dr. Miller grimaced as he tried to shrug the tension from his shoulders. "I'm so damned tired. And it itches under my gloves. I've had no sleep, and I'm no spring chicken myself. I sure hope I'm not getting sick, too."

"I'll keep an eye on the patients if you want to get back to your office and make some calls."

"Thanks. You're the best." Dr. Miller looked at Nurse Crandall, his assistant for the last thirty years. He hoped they'd get through this, but something in his gut said they wouldn't. Maybe he was being paranoid, but he thought he saw some small red spots on her face, likely the start of the signature rash that went with this scourge. He averted his eyes and hoped he was wrong.

He got up, left the tiny hospital ward, and started down the hallway toward his office. He absently wiped a trickle of sweat from near his right temple.

Dr. Miller reached his office, closed the door behind him, then dropped down into his chair and stared at his phone. He picked up the receiver, then set it back down. He'd forgotten to take off his surgical gloves. Too tired, getting too sloppy. He stripped them off—for what it was worth—and turned them inside out in an attempt to keep the surface of his desk from becoming more contaminated than it already was.

Then he put his head in his hands and wept, his sobs wracking his entire exhausted, aged body.

BREAKTHROUGH

CHAPTER 14

Sylvia leaned back in her chair, flexed her shoulders, and rubbed her eyes. She'd been sitting in her personal ResearchStation pod, a minimalist ergonomic cubicle featuring cleanlined work surfaces and storage units all within arm's reach as well as optimally leveled, full-spectrum, nonglare ambient illumination.

Despite the vision-friendly lighting, her eyes ached from staring at the aggregated lab results on her FloaTouch display for the past several hours. No matter how closely she studied the graphs and textual data, the results remained the same.

Total failure.

Not one of the compounds they had tried in the past several weeks had the slightest effect on the MRSA-II organism. She wondered if the Denali people were having the same sort of luck. For Horton's sake, she hoped they were, but for the sake of public health—

"Shouldn't the latest culture and sensitivity be ready by now?" Jerry's voice came from behind her.

She flinched, then turned to find him standing in the doorway to her pod. "Yeah, it should. I just wasn't in a big hurry to go look yet, seeing how the tests have gone so far."

"Well, we might as well find out. If we need to try a new approach, the sooner the better."

Sylvia rose from her chair. "Sure, let's go."

They walked a short distance down the hall to the isolation lab that had been dedicated to their project. A gleaming stainless steel door, inset with a twelve-inch square window of double-paned safety glass, stood before them. To its right, a small retinal scanner hung on the wall. Sylvia leaned over and stared into it with her right eye. A soft beep sounded and the metal door slid open just long enough for her to step inside. It slid shut behind her with a *whoosh*.

Behind the door was a vestibule with cupboards containing disposable full-body hazmat outfits with built-in gloves, overshoes, and head coverings with flexible clear plastic face shields. The outfits left no bit of flesh exposed, and also provided ultramicro air filtration to prevent aerial exposure to lab pathogens. The outfits were stuffy and uncomfortable to wear, but highly effective. Sylvia donned hers, careful to make sure all the seal points were secure before proceeding.

A second sliding metal door and retinal scanner controlled access to the lab itself. Sylvia presented her right eye to the scanner. Another beep sounded and the second door *whooshed* open just long enough for her walk through to the lab.

The lab's interior was roughly the size of a conference room— unlike the old twentieth-century labs that had to accommodate far bulkier equipment, as well as all the lab animals and their supplies. A rectangular work surface, surrounded by several stools, stood in the center of the room. It featured a sink and several Bunsen burners. Shelves of lab glassware lined one wall. Along the other wall stood the most valuable equipment in a modern lab, the multifunction Pathosym III.

Sylvia often wondered how old-school scientists managed in the past, back when every step in the process of developing a new drug required time-consuming, painstaking effort. Not to mention the need for human drug trials in the final testing stages. She just couldn't fathom trying to balance the needs of the testing with the needs of the human subjects. How do you deliberately give one set of people with a deadly disease a candidate drug—and another set a useless placebo? What if the subject drug had unanticipated adverse effects, and killed instead of cured? The Pathosym eliminated all those problems, so she'd never have to make hard ethical choices.

In school, she had trained exclusively on the Pathosym. It provided, in a single piece of equipment, the functionality needed to develop a new drug from start to finish—all in a remarkably compact physical footprint. The entire thing was perhaps five feet across, and rose about three feet up from a desktop-like surface with touch panels and displays built right in. Two rolling ergonomic desk chairs sat before it.

Sylvia took a seat at the Pathosym and quickly checked things over as she waited for Jerry to suit up. The leftmost panel held a dozen one-inch by five-inch hermetically sealed incubator slots. Inside these chambers were glass Petri dishes containing their supply of active, unprocessed colonies of the MRSA-II organism. Indicator lights showed that the colonies were healthy and growing as necessary—for now. It comforted Sylvia to know that, when they were no longer needed, a simple command would destroy them with a blast of intense autoclave-like heat.

The upper set of slots in the center portion of the console was empty. They had already used them to develop a detailed DNA map of the MRSA-II bacteria. That task had taken about twenty minutes.

A feeling of dread descended on Sylvia as her gaze came to rest on the lower central slots, the ones that performed the culture and sensitivity testing against different candidate antibiotic compounds. Sylvia was afraid to check the most recent results, afraid of continued failure to find the right compound.

Avoiding the new C&S results for the moment, she glanced at the rightmost portion of the console and wondered if they would ever progress far enough in this project to use its powerful functionality. In addition to testing the effects of the bacteria itself on humans and various subpopulations, like diabetics, pregnant women, or children, this Pathosym module tested the effects of the bacteria and candidate antibiotic together in a simulated human trial. It provided results in hours rather than years, and with far greater accuracy than ever before possible.

But even with all that power and functionality, so far they'd batted zilch.

Jerry emerged through the sliding metal door, took his seat at the Pathosym, and nodded at Sylvia.

"Well, let's see what it has to say."

Sylvia logged on with a hollow foreboding at the pit of her stomach. She pressed an icon on the touch screen before her, and the latest test results filled the display. Her shoulders slumped as she averted her eyes from the report.

NEGATIVE RESPONSE.

Jerry let out a breath. "Nothing. Absolutely no effect." He hung his head. "I presume you saw the news, right?"

"Yeah. The media did everything they could to avoid calling it an epidemic. But what they described *is* an epidemic, no matter how they want to try to soft-peddle it."

Jerry sat up, his gloved hands clenched into fists. "People are dying. Too damned many people." He turned to Sylvia. Dark circles lay beneath his bloodshot eyes. "And Horton Labs will die, too, unless we think of something soon."

CHAPTER 15

Dan Tremaine sat at his desk and sipped his coffee. Black, strong, and hot. Just as he liked it. Today was going to be a good day. Good for him, good for the president, good for Denali Labs.

Not so good, however, for Horton Drugs. And that made it all the better. He smiled, pressed a tiny button on his PortiComm to activate voice operations, and then said, "Call Vince." He absently fingered the tiny speaker/microphone insert in his left ear as he waited for Vince to pick up.

"Yes, Dan?"

"I just want to verify everything's ready to go on the antibiotic for MRSA-II. You did complete all the testing, right?"

"Yes." Vince cleared his throat, and his tone of voice took on an irritated edge. "I completed all that several months ago. It's been ready to productionalize long before the epidemic got this far."

"That doesn't matter. I had my reasons for delay, and they've paid off. We'll have a lucrative government contract, and the distribution will be taken care of for us. We won't even need to worry about fancy packaging and marketing. The profit margin for this drug will be through the roof. The other fringe benefit is that it will cement Denali's place at the very top of BigPharma. With your profit-sharing arrangement, you stand to rake in plenty of cash yourself, so quit whining about the timing."

Vince sighed and replied more softly. "So what are you going to name this one?"

Dan thought a moment. Usually he put much more time into crafting a name for a new product, calling in focus groups and Marketing. No real need on this one. Demand would be rock solid, no need to pimp it. "Let's call it Lucracillin." He chuckled. "All right, get busy, Vince. I have some calls to make."

He then ordered his PortiComm to call the special private number President Coleridge had given him for the express purpose of providing any progress updates.

"President Coleridge here."

"Mr. President, this is Dan Tremaine. I have important news."

He then explained to a very relieved president that the new antibiotic Lucracillin would provide the cure so desperately needed in the war on MRSA-II. They arranged for the various logistics to be handled, and ended the call.

And now for the best part. Dan made his next call.

"Phil Horton here."

"Hello, Phil. This is Dan Tremaine." He suppressed the wicked laugh that threatened to break free. Barely.

"Yes?"

"I just spoke with the president to let him know the news. We found the cure for MRSA-II, and are now working to begin production and distribution. We're calling our new drug Lucracillin."

After a long pause, Phil uttered a single word as if he had just had the air knocked out of him. "Congratulations."

Dan grinned and took another sip of his coffee. He wasn't quite done. This was too good a moment not to savor. He leaned back in his chair and gazed toward the ceiling before he delivered the rest of the blow. "I suspect this will be the blockbuster that dwarfs all that have come before. Demand will be massive and built-in. We'll have no marketing costs. Distribution will be handled for us. There'll be a profit margin like never before." He waited for a response. Hearing none, he continued. "This ought to put Denali Labs at the very top of BigPharma by any measure you'd care to use."

Again he waited for a response. None came. Then he realized the call had disconnected at some point. He laughed. Maybe Phil Horton didn't have time to chat further. He probably had a lot of work to do— like preparing to wind down his mortally wounded company.

Dan decided a little celebration was in order. He reached inside his top right desk drawer and retrieved a small zippered bag. He unzipped it and laid its contents out on the desk before him: a small mirror, a tiny blade, a disposable straw, and a metal container with a screw-on lid. He opened the container and shook a bit of Stardust onto the mirror. He took pleasure in using the blade to arrange the powder into five nice, even lines.

He bent down and inhaled them, one right after another, using one breath apiece. Then he sat up, closing his eyes and leaning his head back as he savored the sensation of the drug spreading warmth and euphoria throughout his system, into his limbs, into his brain.

Dan felt like he could do anything. No, he *knew* he could do anything. It was good to be Dan Tremaine. Very good indeed.

Phil quietly disconnected the call partway through Dan's boastful rant. He'd congratulated him. That was enough. He didn't feel he needed to have his face rubbed in his failure so Dan Tremaine could stroke his already oversized ego.

Dan's obnoxious self-aggrandizement aside, the truth was this likely signaled the death knell for Horton Drugs unless something really amazing and unexpected happened. Phil felt like he'd just sustained a physical blow to the gut. He'd hardly even had the chance to try to turn things around, and it was probably Game Over already.

Feeling like he'd aged twenty years in the last ten minutes, he pressed a button on his PortiComm and spoke a message for Jerry and Sylvia to come to his office right away. Phil bowed his head and stared down at his desk as he waited for them to join him.

When they showed up at his door, Jerry apologized for them both. "Sorry it took so long. We were in the lab, and had to get out of our hazmat suits. What is it?"

They both wore weary looks as they took their seats and waited. Phil knew they'd been working feverishly over the past weeks to find the MRSA-II cure. But somehow Denali had happened upon it first—and in record time.

Phil struggled to find the words to start off the conversation, then cleared his throat. "I just received a call from Dan Tremaine.

They've found the cure." He sat back in his chair and stared into his lap.

Silence filled the room for several minutes as they all absorbed the news and its implications. Jerry finally broke the spell. "How the hell did they do it? It's been weeks, sure, but that's not that long. Not for a pathogen this vicious and resistant."

Sylvia shook her head. "We haven't found any compound that even touches it. No effect at all. Absolute zero. They must have just stumbled on something. No way could they have run through the usual approaches and found it this quickly."

Phil could hardly bear to see his two best drug developers sitting in front of him, defeated—and especially given the stakes. They'd been beaten in what amounted to an all-or-nothing effort to save the company. He'd have to work hard to see if there was any way to save Horton Drugs despite this setback. He owed that to them, to the company, to his family. But right now, he had no idea how he could make that happen. He ended the discussion as kindly as he could, and sent them on their way for the time being. He couldn't stand to see the pain on their faces.

He needed to be alone to think and he'd damned well better do the best thinking he'd ever done in his life.

CHAPTER 16

Todd set the insulated to-go sack on the passenger seat and took a deep, appreciative whiff of the tangy aroma that wafted out. He'd decided to pick up Sylvia's favorite Chinese food on his way home from the law school. She'd been working so hard lately, he figured she might enjoy a break from cooking. Tonight they could just relax together on the couch, watch a movie, and lazily eat right out of the containers.

For that matter, he, too, wouldn't mind a little break in the routine. The fall semester was hitting the home stretch, and the 1Ls in his Civil Procedure class were starting to get panicky over the looming final exam. He'd endured a virtual stampede of them during his office hours today. They all demanded to know how they could be expected to hold all those rule numbers in their heads for the exam unless they were allowed to have open-book materials.

Of course, soon *he* would be panicking about the final exam, because he still needed to draft the questions—and prepare for the onslaught of grading them all within the school's deadlines. But for tonight, he planned to set that all aside and enjoy some quality time with Sylvia.

Soon he turned into his driveway and pressed the button to open the garage door. As he pulled in, he noticed that Sylvia wasn't yet home. Hopefully she'd arrive soon, or he'd have to zap the food. As advanced as the ZapperBox was over those old microwave ovens, he swore he could still detect a slight degradation to the flavor and texture when cooked food was reheated.

He stepped inside the house, set the bag on the counter and got himself a beer. No sooner did he open it than he heard the growl of the other garage door opening. He opened a beer for Sylvia and handed it to her as she came in.

"Hey, thanks. There's some nice timing." She gave him a kiss, then took a sip.

"Got your favorite from Jade Garden, the Hunan pork."

She glanced over at the counter and noticed the bag. "Oh, what a great idea. I am a little tired tonight."

"I know you've been working your ass off lately. Go ahead and change and get relaxed. I'll take everything out to the living room and we can pick a movie."

"That sounds great." Sylvia gave him another quick kiss and headed upstairs.

Todd took a serving tray from the cupboard and placed the wooden chopsticks, containers of food, a couple of napkins, and their beers on it. He went out into the living room and set it on the coffee table. He flopped down onto the couch, then powered up the entertainment center and left it on the main menu of movie selections.

Sylvia appeared wearing black yoga pants and a pink T-shirt and joined him on the couch. "You go ahead and pick the movie. I'm tired enough I may fall asleep before it's over anyway." She smiled as she removed the paper wrapping from her chopsticks.

Todd waved the remote toward the entertainment center. "We could just listen to music if you'd prefer."

"No, I'd like the distraction of a movie. I just might not make it all the way through."

Todd set down the remote and studied Sylvia's face for a moment before speaking. "Is something wrong? You've been unusually quiet about your work, even though you've been putting in major hours lately."

She avoided eye contact with him as she reached into her container and deftly snagged a piece of pork with her chopsticks. "Well, I've been working on that high-priority project with Jerry for some weeks now, the one to find a cure for MRSA-II."

"And?"

"It hasn't gone well."

"What's the problem?"

"I can't really discuss the project in any more detail than that.

It's confidential. I can tell you I'm pretty sure it was a bet-the-farm project for Horton." She sighed and stared down at her food as she stirred it with her chopsticks. "I'm worried this project's failure might mean the end of the road for Horton."

Todd took her hand. "I didn't realize Horton was in that much trouble. They've been around forever. But you shouldn't be worried about being able to find another position. Your skills are cutting edge. Another drug company would snap you up."

"Yeah, you're probably right about that. But you know, I've only been there a few years, and I really like it there. It has an old-fashioned sort of feel. Not like the cold grind of the larger, newer firms." She popped another bit of pork into her mouth. "But maybe that's the problem. Maybe it's just not possible to compete in the BigPharma arena these days without just being a cold machine of a place."

"We'd be okay on just my salary for a while. You could take your time to find the right fit somewhere else if it comes to that."

"I suppose so. You know, I feel worse for Jerry. He's been there forever. His skills are very, very good, but a little on the old-school side. He might not have such a good landing if Horton were to bite the dust. He's really a good guy." Sylvia shook her head, then looked up at Todd and smiled. "Hey, let's worry about it later. Your food's getting cold. What did you get, anyway?"

"Kung Pao shrimp." Todd unwrapped his chopsticks and plucked a shrimp out of the container. "Good stuff." He grabbed the remote and picked the first action/adventure movie that appeared on the menu. "There. A little escapism for the night."

CHAPTER 17

Phil Horton ended the call with his wife Livvie, then rubbed his temples for a moment to try to dispel some of the tension that had built up there. It would undoubtedly make for a far more pleasant evening for her to have dinner alone than if he were to go home now. Livvie understood him well, and had learned over the years that when he had a tough problem to solve, it was best to let him have his space to focus on it.

He stood, stretched, and went to his window. He gazed out at the parking lot behind the building. Few cars remained in the gathering dusk. Most Horton employees had gone home by now—all but Sylvia and Jerry remained ignorant of the high-stakes gamble they'd lost today.

At least no one would come to his office and bother him. He could think in peace—and he didn't intend to leave his office until he had a plan.

He returned to his desk and took out a fresh legal pad and pen. Despite all the modern computing conveniences, sometimes low-tech worked better for him when he really needed to encourage groundbreaking thought—and God knew he needed some of that tonight.

He went over to his work table and cleared everything from its surface with one sudden, frustrated sweep of his arm. Papers fluttered to the floor around him, but he paid them no heed.

Phil sat in one of the chairs, placed the pad squarely in front of him and took the pen in his hand. He drew a deep breath and faced the blank page. Earlier he had reviewed Horton's monthly revenues and expenses. He had also checked the current reserve balance. He wrote those numbers on the pad and stared down at them.

It didn't take a fancy calculator to see this couldn't go on much longer. Horton was operating seriously in the red each month and had already started to consume the reserves it had built up over the good years. It could go maybe another year at this rate, but probably not much more.

Phil scowled at the bleak numbers on the paper. So what was the true underlying problem? Personnel? Equipment? Management direction? Or just piss-poor luck? Why had the pipeline been so dry for so long? And how the hell did they lose the race with Denali on this project? He clenched the pen in his fist. That would have been the shot in the arm Horton needed. It would have boosted revenues, reserves, and, perhaps most importantly, could have bought time to develop one or more blockbusters to complement it and right the financial ship.

He tapped the pen on the table while he concentrated. He thought back over the last five years in the BigPharma marketplace—and he found himself hard-pressed to think of any blockbusters that weren't Denali's. Why?

Things had been different maybe ten or so years ago. Pathogens used to evolve in a much more gradual way. This made drug development easier, because established drugs could be tweaked in ways to address the evolution. At least usually. Then resistant strains began to develop and they tended to evolve in leaps and bounds. The incremental approach to drugs no longer sufficed.

Then within the last few years, it seemed there were no gradually evolving pathogens left. They were all high-stakes and fast-changing.

And that is when Denali took off, leaving everyone else, including Horton, in the dust. Phil drew a timeline as he contemplated these changes. Then he stopped and stared at what he'd drawn as a connection sparked in his mind.

Was it just coincidence that the dramatic change in pathogens corresponded to the rise of Denali? Was there a cause-and-effect relationship?

And if there was, in which direction did it point? Phil had heard the whispered rumors at BigPharma conferences over the past several years. Until now, he'd just chalked it up to professional jealousy. Looking at the timeline he'd drawn—and considering how quickly Denali had come up with the drug to address the MRSA-II pathogen—he began to wonder. Was it possible? If it was, he had no problem believing that Dan Tremaine would use those methods—or any method for that matter—to get to the top of BigPharma.

He thought about the Pathosym III and its powerful analytical and drug-development capabilities. Maybe it *was* possible. It was at least time to find out.

CHAPTER 18

Jerry took an extra moment to watch Sylvia as she leaned forward and stared intently at a series of charts and graphs on her FloaTouch display. He'd enjoyed working with her on the project, their first together. She made a great partner, with her intelligence and dedication. And, truth be told, he'd enjoyed having the chance to be near her.

But despite their best efforts together, they'd lost the race. It hurt to watch her still trying to make something of their futile work. He cleared his throat, then knocked lightly on the doorway to her ResearchStation pod. "You ready to head over and meet with Phil?"

Sylvia's shoulders slumped as she shut off the display, then swiveled her chair around to face him. Her eyes held the dull, tired look of defeat. "Yeah, sure. Let's go. He's probably going to lay us off. Might as well get it over with."

Jerry had no good comeback to that remark, and so they walked down the hall to Phil's office in tense silence. They hadn't heard a word from Phil since he told them that Denali had beaten them. No news was likely better news than a hastily scheduled meeting.

They announced themselves, entered Phil's office, and took their seats in front of his desk. His wrinkled clothes, disheveled hair, and the dark circles beneath his eyes suggested that he had spent a sleepless night in his office.

Phil ran a hand through his hair in a failed attempt to smooth it into presentability. "I'm sure you're wondering why I called you in, especially given the news I shared with you last time." He stared down at a legal pad that contained what appeared to be diagrams and agitated handwritten notes. "I'll get to the point. Denali's win on the MRSA-II drug was … an enormous blow."

Jerry's stomach tightened as he steeled himself for the inevitable. He'd been with Horton for so long he couldn't picture himself anywhere else. But he'd probably have to. That is, if he could *find* a position somewhere else, given his age and seniority. Companies didn't like to hire older workers, didn't like to pay senior-level salaries when they could get kids fresh out of school with the latest training under their belts. He hoped Horton would be able to pay some sort of severance to help him through what would likely be an extended job search—but given the financials, that might be too much to hope for.

Phil rubbed his eyes. "I spent the night here trying to figure out what to do next. Why are we in this situation, and what can we do to get out of it? And how long can we last while we try?" He tapped his fingers on the legal pad and gazed into the distance as if still pondering the problem.

Jerry stole a quick look at Sylvia. She sat up stiff and straight in her chair, her eyes wide and unblinking. Her pale face wore a look of resignation. He felt bad for her, but at least she would have the easier time finding a new position. She had great skills and excellent credentials. Hell, he'd give her a great reference to anyone who'd ask. He clenched his jaw and wished Phil would get this over with.

"Horton might be able to stagger on under current conditions for about a year. Maybe." Phil stared at them with bloodshot eyes. "Do you want to help me save the company?"

Jerry nodded along with Sylvia, but had no clue how they could save the floundering Horton at this point, given the deadly combination of dire financials and Denali's huge win.

Phil leaned forward in his chair, his face animated with newfound energy. "All right, then. How far did you get on the MRSA-II project?"

"Well, we developed maybe a dozen compounds." Sylvia sighed. "But none of them had any effect on the pathogen."

"Good. That's good." Phil stood, went to his window, and stared outside. "Last night I figured out why Denali won—and why they've been winning as they have."

Jerry exchanged a confused glance with Sylvia, and wondered if he dared hope for their jobs and Horton's survival after all.

Phil turned back around to face them. "I looked at it all different ways, and I kept coming back to the same conclusion. There have been rumors that I didn't believe. I didn't *want* to believe them. Now we have no choice but to beat them at their own game."

Something squirmed in the pit of Jerry's stomach as he realized where Phil was going with this.

"I am convinced that Tremaine's business model is to design pathogens—and their cures—and so create his own markets, his own blockbusters." Phil rushed over to his desk, picked up the legal pad and slapped it for emphasis. "How else can you explain how fast they grew? How fast they came up with blockbuster after blockbuster?" He threw the pad back down onto his desk. "And how fast he came up with the drug for MRSA-II?"

Sylvia muttered, "Oh my God."

"I don't want to stoop to Tremaine's level, but it's life or death for Horton. I tried—believe me I tried—to think of other alternatives, but I see no other choice." He faced them again, his jaw set. "I want you to alter the MRSA-II organism in such a way that it is susceptible to one of the compounds you developed. Gene-splicing, whatever it takes. Be sure it's a solid cure, though. I don't want to create a monster, just a pathogen-cure pairing that will buy us some market share."

Jerry sat speechless. In all his years at Horton, no CEO would ever have considered such a thing. Horton Drugs had always stood for the highest ethics, even when those around them might have bent the rules. Horton had never had a scandal of any kind, never any regulatory action against it—even back when the FDA had some teeth.

Phil dropped into his chair as if all his energy had suddenly fled. "So, can we do it?"

Sylvia scowled down into her lap with a look of concentration, then spoke slowly, as if reluctantly reaching a decision. "I think so. I need to think through the most efficient approach, but yes, I think it can be done."

"Phil, I—" Stunned and disappointed with both Phil and

Sylvia and their willingness to cast aside ethics for dollars, Jerry struggled to find the right words. "I'm not sure this is the best way to go. Horton Drugs—"

Phil slapped his palms onto his desk and glared at him. "Do you want to keep your job?" He swept his arm horizontally to indicate the entire building. "Do you want *all* of us to keep our jobs? For Horton to even survive? Because that's what it's come down to. I'm well aware of Horton's heritage, thank you. And I'm not happy about having to do this, either. So we do it as carefully as possible. But we do it. Am I clear?"

CHAPTER 19

Sylvia felt like she'd just been picked up and dropped off into a new reality. She'd been sure they were going to get their pink slips, and instead Phil had revealed a theory and a plan that she was still trying to process.

As they stepped outside Phil's office and shut the door, Jerry turned to her, his face white and his lips pressed tightly together. "We need to talk."

"What—"

"What do you think? Let's go to the conference room where it's private."

They walked the short distance down the hall without another word, then Jerry motioned her into the room ahead of him and closed the door.

Sylvia took a seat and watched as Jerry glared at the floor and strode back and forth, his jaw and fists clenched. She'd never seen him so worked up; he was always calm and even-tempered. She waited for him to speak.

Finally, he stopped and faced her. "I can't believe he wants to do this."

"Well, you heard him. Horton's going down unless something drastic is done. That's not inside information, you know. The stock price has been in the tank for the last few years. I just can't believe what Denali's been doing."

Hands in pockets, Jerry began to pace again. "I'd have expected this if they'd brought in an outsider, but a family member who would even entertain an idea like this … given the history here."

Wanting to put an end to the conversation, Sylvia stood.

"Don't get me wrong, Jerry. I don't like the ethics of it either, but if Phil's right—and I suspect he is, now that I think about it—Denali has changed the landscape so there is no other way to compete. Else, you might as well hand Denali the entire BigPharma market, because that's what will happen." She shook her head. "It's sad, but Denali appears to have set the standard for our line of work forever."

"It's *wrong*, Sylvia. It's just wrong."

She cut him off and spoke through clenched teeth. "I don't disagree with you. But we can't afford to live in the past. Horton has to adapt to survive. But we must make sure we do it in the safest possible way. I'll need your help to crosscheck at every stage. I wouldn't want to miss anything—there's too much at stake."

Jerry flopped into a chair and put his face in his hands. "I never dreamed I'd be in this position—having to do something morally loathsome to keep my job. If this is going to be the norm going forward, I need to consider a new career. God knows what, but I don't want to work this way. It's not why I went into this line of work."

Sylvia realized how deeply Phil's plan disturbed Jerry and regretted snapping at him. She softened her tone. "You've put a lot into this company, I know. Maybe if this works and Horton gets back on its feet, Phil might not have to play by Denali's rules going forward. Let's create a new pathogen. But let's do it together, carefully. Let's create one that's contagious enough to fuel a blockbuster drug, but that isn't dangerous. Something that's just really annoying and inconvenient to contract."

Jerry sighed and stared down at the table. He spoke in a resigned tone. "I suppose that's the best compromise under the circumstances. Maybe if we succeed, Phil won't feel pressured to make this the new business model going forward." He shrugged and avoided eye contact with her. "We can hope so, anyway."

CHAPTER 20

Vince Calhoun took his seat in the crowded auditorium fifteen minutes before the appointed time. He glanced around as he waited, while the overhead lights were still on full strength. Everyone from the lowliest grunt lab assistants to the board of directors was in attendance at the quarterly all-staff meeting.

True believers all around. And why not? Everyone around him had benefitted handsomely from Denali stock options. Denali had never had a bad quarter in its relatively brief history.

The public, the pundits, anyone you might ask would say the same thing. Dan Tremaine is a genius, an innovator. A force to be reckoned with who changed the world of BigPharma in only a few short years.

Yep, he sure as hell was all those things. Vince knew this for a fact. As lead scientist and Tremaine's confidante, Vince knew more than the CFO did about why Denali was so successful. He knew firsthand of Tremaine's consuming ambition and single-minded focus on doing whatever it took to put Denali at the top. Tremaine had innovated, all right. He'd hatched the idea of making his own markets, and Vince had made the idea operational.

They'd started small, with pathogens they tweaked from existing lines. They were similar enough to other organisms that it didn't take much to develop the needed companion drugs. And the similarity to other known pathogens helped hide their strategy, because it suggested natural evolution and adaptation—rather than the hand of deliberate design—was at work.

Vince had been fine with that approach. There was little downside or risk, and plenty of upside. The diseases weren't that severe, and their scheme was unlikely to be discovered. The strategy had worked as intended, and it put Denali in a very strong financial position very quickly.

But that wasn't enough for Tremaine. He wanted the big win. So he'd raised the ante considerably in asking Vince to develop a mutant version of the extremely dangerous flesh-eating MRSA bacterium.

Despite his misgivings, Vince undertook the project and made damned sure he also developed a compound that was a safe and rock-solid cure. Then, under instructions from Tremaine, he'd planted samples of the pathogen in several key locations. He'd expected Denali to release the cure shortly after cases of MRSA-II began to emerge. Tremaine's insistence on waiting until the disease spread widely enough to force the president's hand surprised him and created an ongoing conflict that had damaged their previously congenial relationship.

But, once again, Tremaine had made the nervy call and won big—even if more people than necessary died because of it. Vince hoped this would be enough of a win for Tremaine to dial it back a bit. But, knowing Tremaine, it would likely only stoke his ambitions.

The lights dimmed and the stage curtain opened. A single spotlight highlighted the emcee at the podium. He wore a formal tux for today's event. Another thing that always made Vince uncomfortable—though it now paled in comparison to how the MRSA-II situation had been orchestrated—was the way Tremaine presented himself as a sort of rock star. Sure, the company was successful, partly due to his ideas. But his ideas would have been nothing if Vince hadn't been able to execute them for him. All these things rankled Vince, though he sure as hell couldn't complain about his financial share of the success.

After the emcee said a few words and extended his arm to invite Tremaine onto the stage, the audience reacted by giving a standing ovation. Vince rose along with them, not wanting to look out of place.

Dan Tremaine stepped up to the podium. His proud bearing and the confident look on his face gave the impression of a man fully aware he was at the top of his game. After enjoying several minutes of thunderous applause, he motioned for everyone to sit so he could speak.

"This quarter marks a new milestone in the history of Denali Labs. We've entered into what will undoubtedly prove to be our most lucrative product launch *ever.*" He paused for effect as he glanced at the expectant faces in the audience.

"Denali Labs took on what is arguably *the* most dangerous bacterial pathogen of modern times, MRSA-II, and succeeded in finding a cure. Not only did we find the cure before any of our so-called peers, but we signed an exclusive distribution contract with the U.S. government that will ensure blockbuster-level sales for the foreseeable future. All this with minimal production costs on our part, because the government is handling all the packaging and distribution." He paused and smiled. "Sorry, Marketing. You don't have any work to do for this product. Lucracillin will sell itself!"

The audience erupted into enthusiastic applause and again rose to its feet. Vince couldn't decide if he was more proud of having developed such a drug, or more disgusted at how the whole scenario had been set up. He stood and clapped as he wondered how many people died during the extended delay Tremaine had demanded.

But even if Tremaine had listened to him and kept the cure's launch time to an absolute minimum, the pathogen was so deadly that some deaths would have been unavoidable during the time needed to establish the disease as an identifiable problem. As it was, though, Tremaine's delay had come dangerously close to creating an uncontrollable epidemic that even the most efficient possible drug distribution scenario might not have been able to stem.

That was a scenario Vince didn't want to envision. He returned his attention to Tremaine's speech.

"Lucracillin will certainly cement Denali's position at the very top of BigPharma. No other company will be able to touch our sales and our success. All others, including the old and venerable Horton Drugs, will wither and die. *We* will control the entire market for drugs to combat bacterial pathogens." He paused. "And how does it feel to be a part of that success?" He held his arms open wide and smiled broadly.

The applause became deafening.

CHAPTER 21

Dr. Lydia Erickson swept aside the privacy curtain in the ER's staging area. A young girl about six years old lay in the bed, her face flushed with fever and already riddled with the open sores typical of MRSA-II. Her mother sat hunched in a chair next to the bed. Both mother and daughter shared the same terrified expression and looked dangerously close to outright panic.

"Doctor, can you help my little girl?" The question came out in a fragile whisper.

"Let me take a look." Dr. Erickson donned a disposable microbe-screening mask that covered her nose and mouth, took the child's pulse with a gloved hand, then peered more closely at the facial lesions. "I'll need to run a culture and sensitivity to verify, but I'm nearly certain it's MRSA-II."

The mother gasped as all color drained from her face. "Oh, no …"

"Don't worry. We have a new medication for it that's extremely effective. I'll start her on it right away while we wait for the lab results, just to give her a head start."

Dr. Erickson gently cradled the child's face. "Don't worry, honey, this will only take a second." She swabbed a lesion before the girl had time to react and placed the sample in a glass tube, then turned to the anxious mother. "I'm quite sure we're dealing with MRSA-II here. I've seen plenty of it in the last several months. It's pretty distinctive."

The mother's shoulders slumped with relief. "Thank you, Doctor."

Dr. Erickson drew the curtain closed, removed her gloves

and mask, then accessed the girl's medical record on the electronic wall panel. She tapped the touch screen to order the necessary blood tests, entered her initial diagnosis, and set up the prescription for Lucracillin.

She left the triage area to go take a little break before examining the next half dozen patients who had come in while she was examining the last two. At this rate, she'd never catch up. As she entered the break room to get some coffee, she saw Dr. Gabe Lemoli slumped in a chair at one of the tables.

"Hey, Gabe. How long've you been here today? You look worn out."

"Thanks for the compliment, Lydia."

"Anytime."

"I'm actually in my second consecutive shift. Been here all night. I don't think we've quite seen the crest of the MRSA-II problem."

"It's slowing some since they released the Lucracillin, don't you think?" Lydia pressed a button on the machine and a steaming cup of fresh coffee materialized within seconds. She took the cup in both hands and savored the relaxing warmth.

"Yeah, I think so. It's definitely decelerating, but we've got a ways to go before I'd call it under control. That Lucracillin is great. I haven't lost a single patient since it came out." Gabe rubbed his forehead with one hand as he sipped a bit of his cold coffee. "But like all wonder drugs, it sets up some bad behaviors, and I think that's prolonging the epidemic."

Lydia sat across from him and sipped her coffee. "How so?"

"Well, the media's been gushing over its efficacy. And rightly so. I haven't seen an antibiotic this effective against such a stubborn pathogen in, well, I don't remember how long. But that's the problem." He extended his hand toward her, palm up, as he made his case. "The general public hears that and figures with an easy cure available, they can let their guard down. Before the drug came out, people were more careful about exposure. Now they don't seem to care and I think that's why the numbers haven't tapered faster."

"Damned good point, Gabe. Before Lucracillin came out, large public events were cancelled, people were staying home.

Everybody's acting like everything is back to normal now, and that does seem a little premature. At least we have an effective cure now, but still ... prevention is always better. It's tough on the infrastructure to admit all these patients—and tough on us, too."

Gabe leaned back in his chair and moved his head from side to side to flex the tightness from his neck. "I think we'll get it eradicated. It'll just take longer this way." He took another sip of his coffee, grimaced, and set it aside. "You know, I'll bet everyone at Denali Labs is thrilled the public has let their guard down. Just that much more in sales for them."

"I'm sure they're laughing all the way to the bank. I'll bet this single drug breaks all sales records before this is over." Lydia finished her coffee. "Well, I'd better get back to it. You should go home, Gabe. There'll be patients enough for you on your next shift. Get some rest."

Gabe ran a hand through his hair. "I'll think about it. Take care, Lydia."

Dr. Erickson headed back to the triage area and checked the electronic status board outside the door. Another four patients had checked in just during her brief break. She took a deep breath and readied herself. This was going to be a long shift.

CHAPTER 22

President Coleridge pointed at one of the flat panels on the Oval Office wall. It displayed a real-time line graph of the number of new MRSA-II cases reported since the outbreak began. The line trended steadily downward since the peak several weeks ago. "It's working. Whatever Tremaine and his people at Denali did, they did it right." He smiled and turned to his secretary of HHS, John Humphrey. It felt like the first time he'd smiled in weeks—and it probably was.

"It's impressive, to be sure. But I think we deserve a good share of the credit. We activated widespread distribution of the drug at a speed never thought possible. Both factors in concert contributed to the launch's success."

"You're right, John. Wouldn't matter how effective Lucracillin was if we hadn't gotten it out to even the most remote parts of the Homeland as quickly as we did." The president leaned back in his massive leather chair. "And they say the government can't mobilize anything effectively." He allowed himself a smirk.

John chuckled. "This can't hurt your re-election chances."

"True enough. Never too early to think about that." He gazed toward the ceiling as he considered possible themes for his next campaign. "I can run as the president who brought MRSA-II to its knees and reinvigorated the country."

President Coleridge shifted his gaze back to John and refocused on his more immediate concern. "This thing put the Homeland in serious danger. People quit going out to buy things. The market was in the crapper. The economy can only take so much of that. Fortunately, things are back on track already. Market's near an all-time high, in fact."

"I don't want to think about what would have happened if we hadn't gotten this thing under control as quickly as we did."

"I don't, either." The president cleared his throat and leaned forward. "So, as great as this news is, it's not why I asked you here today."

John straightened in his chair, ready to listen. "Yes, sir. What do you want to discuss?"

"This whole incident gives me grave concerns about Homeland Security. We don't know where this bug came from, do we? Did it just develop, or did an enemy agency plant it? Was it meant to be just a message—or was it meant to destroy the Homeland?"

"I … don't know. Do you have anyone at the CIA looking into that?"

"Not yet. I will, though. The crisis was too emergent to spend time looking for causes. We needed to stop the bleeding first. And it may have been a natural development, who knows?"

"Yes, it certainly could have been. We set the stage for the evolution of more and more resistant strains of bacteria years ago by using antibiotics for every little infection and in agriculture to increase production." He shook his head. "Damned bugs just got better and better at beating our drugs."

"But what if an enemy *did* plant it? The epidemic was, after all, confined to the Homeland. It could happen again."

"I wouldn't necessarily assume it was planted here. It could have started here from some random mutation, and just hadn't jumped borders yet. Thank God."

"Hard to know, but we have to err on the side of paranoia. We have many enemies. Whether naturally occurring or intentional, this could happen again. What do we do?"

"Isn't the answer obvious? Call Tremaine up. I'm not being facetious. He's proven he can deal with this sort of thing. And we know we can handle large-scale distribution."

The president rubbed his temple lightly with his right forefinger as he considered how best to introduce the next topic. "This has made me think of something else, as well."

"What's that?"

He looked John Humphrey in the eye. "This doesn't go beyond these doors, understood?"

John nodded. "Of course, sir."

"Some day we might need to develop a pathological strain for our own purposes—either as a counterterrorism measure or as a first-strike measure if the situation warranted it."

John paled and remained silent.

"We'd need the capability to develop such an organism, as well as the capability to develop a cure that could be distributed to offer protection to the *appropriate* populations."

"I ... hadn't thought about that, sir. It takes all my focus to deal with the public health issues that just naturally arise."

"I understand this is outside your normal area of expertise. I plan to confer with those more grounded in this sort of thing as well. But if we initiate something along these lines, I'd like you to be involved because of your experience on this project. Your knowledge would be transferable and helpful to such a team."

"Of course, sir. Whatever you need."

"Good, John. I knew I could count on you." The president smiled. It was good to have staff who understood the importance of cooperation.

CHAPTER 23

Sylvia tapped the command icon on the Pathosym III's control panel and held her breath a moment as she waited for it to respond. "Jerry! We got it!"

Jerry hopped off his lab stool and rushed over to view the results. He let out a low whistle. "It worked. Thank God."

"Wasn't God this time, it was you. You're far better at gene splicing than I am. That's why I let you have the honors."

"That's not what I meant. You know how I feel about tinkering with that MRSA-II beast. It scares me. I'd just as soon burn all our specimens up in the autoclave so they didn't survive another moment. I was worried that our splice might have unintended consequences. We wanted to combine the contagious nature of MRSA-II and the disease profile and sensitivity to our compound of the other pathogen."

Jerry flopped into the other chair in front of the Pathosym console. "Can you imagine if we'd gotten it wrong and it was neither sensitive to our compound, nor to Lucracillin?"

"I see what you mean. But we were pretty confident we'd identified the correct genes to splice." Sylvia glanced again at the display, just to make sure she'd read the results correctly. "You're right, though. It's tricky stuff and we could have gotten it wrong."

Jerry's tone took on a sarcastic edge. "Yep, we're so damned clever, now we've created a whole new pathogen of our very own. We still need to run the human modeling tests to confirm the disease profile and interaction between the pathogen and our compound in the human body. I'm nowhere near ready to feel at ease yet. Not till after the human modeling results."

"No time like the present." Ignoring Jerry's tone, Sylvia transferred a petri dish of the new pathogen from an incubator slot to a modeling module slot. No antibiotic had been introduced into that colony so it could be tested solely to determine the symptoms it would cause. She tapped several command icons and sat back in her chair. "All right. Let's see what it says."

They both waited in awkward silence for the twenty minutes it took for the Pathosym to complete the modeling analysis. As they waited, Sylvia wondered what it must have been like for Jerry and other old-school scientists to have to wait weeks to learn what symptoms a particular pathogen produced. Human trials were just so primitive.

A subdued tone sounded, signaling the test's completion. They both locked their eyes on the display as it listed the symptoms one could expect from an infection with their newly designed pathogen.

Sylvia let out a held breath. "That's a relief."

"It certainly is. We couldn't have asked for a better profile. The disease will be highly contagious, but will only cause vague, annoying flu-like symptoms, some gastrointestinal distress, and minor lesions on the skin. Nothing nearly as serious as its daddy." Jerry pushed back his chair and rubbed his temples through his hazmat suit. "Now we just need to know if, in the human body, the compound cures without significant side effects."

"Ask and you shall receive." Sylvia took another petri dish of the pathogen, introduced some of the antibiotic compound, and inserted the dish into the module that modelled drug and pathogen interactions in the human body. The Human Drug Trial in a Box, as the Pathosym marketing folks liked to call it.

Again they sat in expectant silence for the twenty minutes it took the Pathosym to complete the test. A vague feeling of superstition intruded at the edge of Sylvia's mind as she waited. After total defeat in the competition with Denali, their work on this project had been going almost flawlessly. How long could that last before something went wrong?

Another hushed tone sounded, and they both peered at the report presented on the display. Sylvia's sense of foreboding intensified. The results were just too good to be true.

Jerry pushed back his chair, then stood. "Time to quit while we're ahead. A projected 99.99% efficacy rate, with a .01% chance of diarrhea as the drug's only side effect. That's about the best we can hope for in our first shot at playing God. I hope Phil will be pleased that the disease will be quite contagious and damned annoying to come down with, and so the drug is likely to be the blockbuster Horton needs."

"Hey, what do you say we shut it down for the day and have a drink to celebrate? My treat." Sylvia genuinely liked Jerry and wished he weren't quite so disturbed by this project. She wasn't happy about it either, but his reluctance forced her into taking the lead—which probably just added to the friction between them.

He weighed the idea for a few seconds before answering. "Well, all right. Thanks."

CHAPTER 24

"I think the time is right *now*." Dan Tremaine set aside the tiny silver tray of Stardust, rose from his chair, and paced the length of his office like a caged panther.

Vince Calhoun hated it when Dan got into this sort of mood. He'd acted like a maniac since the day he founded Denali, but whenever he had a victory under his belt—let alone a little Stardust—he became intolerable.

And with the Lucracillin triumph, Dan's ego had burgeoned like never before.

Vince suppressed a grimace and tried to speak in a calm, rational manner, for what it was worth. "I really think we ought to hold off for a little while. The MRSA-II epidemic is only now easing off. Don't we want to be sure things don't take an unexpected turn before we introduce anything new?"

Dan waved a dismissive hand and kept on pacing. "Oh come on, we can rely on our enhanced Pathosym. Its models didn't indicate any significant tendency for the MRSA-II organism to mutate, right? The distribution pipeline is in full swing, so Lucracillin is readily available for anyone contracting the disease. We've waited long enough."

Vince hesitated to raise his other concern, anticipating Dan's likely response. "There's something else."

Dan stopped pacing, folded his arms across his chest, and fixed a glare on Vince. "What?"

"Well, don't you think the extreme visibility of the MRSA-II outbreak combined with the rather quick release of Lucracillin might ... raise some questions?"

"About what? You think it might raise suspicions that we

developed both the disease and the cure?" Dan shrugged. "Who says other BigPharma companies haven't done it, too? Just not as well as we have."

"There've been rumors floating around for some time, but no one's ever come out and accused anyone. Until now, the pathogens we've been launching were relatively mild and not terribly distinctive. Their spread wasn't constant front-page news like it's been with MRSA-II." He twisted his hands in his lap. "And the president didn't get involved like he did this time. What if he started wondering if we found the cure first because *we* created the pathogen and had everything all set up from the outset?"

Dan stomped over to his desk and slammed down his fist, nearly knocking over the Stardust. "The *president*? Do you have any idea how much I've contributed to his campaign fund over the years—both in the name of Denali Labs and from my personal funds?" He stabbed an angry finger toward Vince. "No, he knows who his supporters are, and he knows who his *best* supporters are. The next election is too close for him to even consider biting the hand that feeds him. We have nothing to fear from him."

Vince considered this for a moment, and found he couldn't refute Dan's currency-driven logic. Money meant speech and access—even for corporations these days. Perhaps *especially* for corporations. "I suppose you're right. I hadn't thought of it that way."

"So, we need to start working on the next blockbuster. Question is, how do we top this one?" Dan smiled as he gazed off into the distance and considered the possibilities.

"Do we really need to top this one? We could develop some other workhorse-type drug as we have in the past. That would provide good solid revenue growth without the additional risk."

"What risk? We've specifically modified our Pathosym to support this business model. It provides all the analysis we could possibly need—accurately, and way faster than the base model ever could."

"I don't doubt the reliability of the Pathosym's modeling. It's not that. I've told you before, I think we took a terrible risk in waiting for the epidemic to reach the proportions it did just to attract the president's attention. MRSA-II is an extremely aggressive pathogen, and it could have—and nearly did—get out of hand before the drug became generally available."

"But look at what we got from waiting that we wouldn't otherwise have gotten." Dan counted on his fingers to drive home his point. "Free—and massive—distribution. No need to spend a dime on marketing. The fastest FDA approval on record—even with the new streamlined process. Sales of Lucracillin are nearly pure profit! What better scenario could you possibly want?"

"I won't argue with you there. But what if the epidemic had gotten out of control before the distribution channels were ready? What then?"

"Well it didn't, and that's what matters. Get started on the next project. I want another blockbuster—even better than this one. We can talk about timing considerations after we review the new pathogen's profile. So stop the excuses and get busy, Vince." Dan sat down and waved his arm in a dismissive gesture. Then he leaned over to snort up another line of Stardust.

Vince stood and left the room without another word. He didn't dare utter what he really wanted to say to Dan.

CHAPTER 25

Sylvia cleared the dishes from the dinner table, then went to join Todd in the living room. A nice, quiet evening and an early bedtime would suit her just fine.

"What are you in the mood for tonight?" Todd picked up the remote, powered up the entertainment center, and accessed the scrolling list of movie choices.

Sylvia let out a muffled groan when she saw the listing for the latest thriller movie: *Outbreak III*. Way too close to home.

"Not into watching a movie tonight? Are you okay?"

Sylvia waved her hand. "No, I'm fine. Just trying to get work out of my mind."

Todd set down the control and turned to her. "Sylvia, what's going on? Last time we talked about it, you were worried about your project—and about Horton. Are things getting better, or not?"

She tucked her legs up, wrapped her arms around them, and rested her chin on her knees. "The bet-the-farm project—the first one—ended some weeks ago. We didn't succeed."

"What's Horton going to do?"

"Well, that was the first bet-the-farm project."

"There's more?"

Sylvia hesitated as she struggled with how much to reveal. She'd been sworn to secrecy on the competition with Denali because of the president's involvement, but she hadn't specifically been told to maintain that level of secrecy on the new project. She presumed she shouldn't talk about it casually, but Todd was a lawyer. He knew how to keep confidences. And he was her husband now.

"Yeah, I'm working on a new project with Jerry. If it works

as we're hoping, it could save Horton Drugs."

"Sounds important. What is it?" Todd smiled. "Or can you explain it so a mere layman like me can understand?"

"It's confidential, so you can't breathe a word of it to anyone else."

Todd held up his hand, Boy Scout-style. "Okay."

"We're coming up with a new drug." She paused, then decided to trust Todd with the whole truth. "And the pathogen it will act on."

A frown creased Todd's face as he grasped the implications of what she'd said. "*What?*"

"Phil says Horton can't remain operational for much longer—the finances are that bad. So we need to come up with a blockbuster drug. Quickly." Sensing Todd's building anger, she stared down at her knees before continuing. "We can't wait for a new disease to arise and then try to find a cure for it."

"So you're designing your *own?*" Todd's jaw hung open as he awaited her answer.

"'Fraid so." She squared her shoulders and looked him in the eye. "There's been scuttlebutt for years that the more successful BigPharma companies have already engaged in this sort of business model, at least once in a while. I don't know if it's true." She shrugged one shoulder. "I have to wonder about Denali Labs, though. They've risen way too fast. I especially wonder about Lucracillin and the MRSA-II bacterium." She gazed across the room as she thought about it some more, then spoke softly, as if to herself. "No, that would have been too risky."

Todd put his hand on her shoulder. "Do you hear what you're saying? Even if other companies have done this, how can you defend the ethics, even to save Horton?"

"Well ... I ... can't, entirely. But we're being very careful to develop something that isn't dangerous, just readily transmitted and annoying enough to create a high enough demand for the curing drug to get Horton back on its feet."

"How the hell are you managing to do that?"

Sylvia glanced at Todd and did not like the look on his face. It made her feel like some sort of criminal.

"Look, it's not like we don't understand pathogens and how to analyze them. We wouldn't release something dangerous. We have equipment that accurately models everything we need to know. We selected a bacteria that was sensitive to a drug we already developed, and we spliced its genes into the MRSA-II organism. According to the models, we got exactly what we wanted: a pathogen with the ready transmission of MRSA-II, with non-life-threatening symptoms, that is readily cured by the compound we already developed—with only the mildest of side effects."

"It's that easy, and nothing can go wrong?" Todd folded his arms and sat back, physically distancing himself from her.

"Our equipment's modeling functionality has never been inaccurate."

Todd held up his right hand, palm toward her. "Okay, I'm not a scientist. I don't have your training. I'll admit that. But this makes me terribly nervous that something will go wrong. Not only that, it's so deceptive and, frankly, *unethical* to create demand for your product by developing a pathogen. That is just not right."

"What am I supposed to do, Todd? Horton has to stay competitive, or it will close down. In all likelihood, we're just doing what others have already done, only we're taking pains to minimize the risk to the public by developing such a benign pathogen."

"A *benign* pathogen? How did you just say that with a straight face?"

"Quit twisting things. You know what I mean."

"I heard you. I just can't believe you would participate in something like this." Todd stood. "I'm going to take a shower. I need to get in early tomorrow for a meeting. I can't quite wrap my head around all this right now." He turned his back to her and headed upstairs.

Sylvia remained on the couch, stung by Todd's anger. She was uncomfortable with the project herself and expected it would concern Todd as well, but she hadn't expected such a vehement response. She put her head in her hands and sat like that until it sounded like Todd had turned in before she went upstairs to bed.

CHAPTER 26

"Let's check everything over one more time before we go see Phil, okay?" Jerry used their meeting later that morning as an excuse for yet another compulsive check of the test results. Deep in his heart, he feared they had missed something crucial, something that would come back to haunt them at some later date.

Sylvia let out an impatient sigh. "We've already checked and rechecked. The results haven't changed. But if it will make you feel better ..." She tapped a few control icons to display all the test results as they huddled in her ResearchStation pod.

Jerry peered over her shoulder, hoping that two sets of eyes would be absolutely certain to miss nothing, not even the smallest detail. No amount of checking could possibly suffice for what they were trying to do.

She scooted her chair aside to give him a better view of the display. "See? Same as before. Flu-like effects, GI distress, and possibly minor skin lesions that would last five to seven days. Just enough to disrupt work and personal lives and create demand for a fast-acting cure, but not enough to cause hospitalizations and major complications—even for vulnerable individuals. See, the drug will be 99.999% effective at the dosage the computer determined, with a .01% chance of mild diarrhea as the only side effect. And the disease will be plenty contagious." She sat back in her chair and folded her arms. "It's everything you could ask for—and the report hasn't changed since the last time you wanted to check."

"Very funny."

"I wasn't trying to be funny. I know you're not comfortable

with this. But we've done everything possible to minimize risk and still achieve the goal."

"I guess. I just can't believe Horton Drugs has had to stoop to something this low to stay in business. It's just not how things are done here."

Sylvia whirled in her chair to face him. "Get over it! Sometimes I get really tired of hearing about the good old days, all right? The world is the way it is now. Our competition has likely been doing this for some time—and probably with much riskier pathogens than we're planning to use. It's a matter of survival, and Horton has to change with the times, or just fucking *die*."

Jerry sat silent, wounded by Sylvia's words. She had never spoken to him like that before. He had thought she at least respected him for his lengthy experience, even if she would probably never find him attractive or return his feelings for her. Instead she seemed to think he was just some old guy who lived in the past and couldn't keep up. He decided it best to say nothing further about it.

Maybe he should retire and leave this all behind, if she was right about the new rules of survival. This was not a world he wanted to be a part of.

Phil Horton fidgeted at his desk, hoping Jerry and Sylvia would bring him good news today. He'd had no news of the welcome variety in quite some time. Just yesterday he'd learned of a major unexpected expense he could ill afford. One of the buildings on campus had developed a roof leak that had led to an expensive mess in one of the production areas. What a joy it was to try to run a large company that was already in trouble when he took the reins. Not something he'd ever aspired to, that's for sure.

They arrived at the scheduled time, both looking tight-lipped and tense as they took their seats. He prepared himself for some more bad news. "Well, how is the project going?"

Sylvia spoke without so much as a glance at Jerry. "We've created a new pathogen and its curing drug that meet all your requirements." She proceeded to provide additional detail. "We've checked the results multiple times. Looks solid."

Phil sat back in his chair, ran a hand through his hair, and let out a long breath. He felt like at least some of the weight had been taken from his shoulders, and that there might just be a hope of saving Horton after all. "Great work. Thank you. This sounds like precisely what we need. Jerry, you've been uncharacteristically quiet. Do you have anything to add?"

He stared at the floor as he answered. "No. I don't. Sylvia summed it all up just fine."

"All right. I'll make sure we'll be ready to manufacture and distribute the drug when the time comes. However, given the situation, the sequence of steps to production is going to be, well, unusual. First, we need to figure out how to release the pathogen into the population so the disease becomes emergent. Once it becomes an identified disease, then we must decide how long to make it appear that we're working on a cure. Then we present it to the FDA for fast-track approval and start marketing, manufacturing and distribution." He stared at his desktop for a moment. "Sure feels strange to do it this way."

Both Sylvia and Jerry remained silent. Jerry appeared to be shaking his head ever so slightly.

"So—how to get it out there. Any thoughts?"

"We hadn't worked that part out yet. I'll take the lead."

"Thank you, Sylvia. Let me know when you have a plan and we can discuss it."

"Certainly."

"Thanks again, both of you." Phil couldn't help but notice the apparent tension between Sylvia and Jerry. He wondered what the problem might be, then decided he had enough to worry about. They could work it out themselves, whatever it was.

THE RELEASE

CHAPTER 27

Sylvia sat alone in the lab and worked on her plan all after-noon. Jerry had been avoiding her since their argument after meeting with Phil last week. She'd never encountered such behavior in a professional environment, and wasn't quite sure how to react to it. On the one hand, she could really use his expertise in vetting ideas. But on the other hand, he seemed to think he had the market cornered on ethics, and any interaction with him would be fraught with tension and antagonism that she didn't need right now.

She set aside the conflict with Jerry and focused on the immediate problem of how to get the new pathogen out into the world. She knew she had to do it herself, not entrust it to someone who wasn't in on the project. But how could she do it effectively and not get caught?

The pathogen had to be released someplace where it would likely infect a core set of people who would in turn act as prolific, unknowing vectors for further distribution. That was the key. With its contagion profile, it should take off from there. Sylvia stared into space as she sat before the Pathosym console and ran through various ideas in her head. Then she slapped her hand down on the table. She knew what she needed to do.

Sylvia went to the supply cabinet at the far end of the lab and looked inside. She selected a half dozen sealed sterile swabs and an equal number of resealable plastic transportation sheathes. The sheathes would allow her to transport the swabs once she loaded them with the pathogen.

She returned to the Pathosym where she kept several colonies of the new pathogen incubating. With gloved hands, she removed one of the glass petri dishes. One by one, she opened a fresh swab, collected a sample, and then sealed the swab in its individual sheath, taking care not to contaminate the sheath's outer surface. When she was done, she put the petri dish back in the Pathosym's incubator chamber, let out a long breath, and flexed her shoulders to relieve the tension that had built up. She gazed down at the neat row of sealed swabs on the counter. Carried this way, they were completely safe. For now.

CHAPTER 28

"What are you doing?" Todd appeared in the door of Sylvia's home office with a puzzled look on his face. He was dressed and ready to leave for school.

"Oh, I was just checking the bus schedule."

"Why? You never take the bus."

"Well, I need to go downtown for a meeting today, and I didn't want to hassle with parking." She hoped Todd would buy her story and drop the subject. As if it wasn't bad enough at work with the tension between her and Jerry, a distinct chill had settled into her home life since her argument with Todd about the project. She had too much on her mind this morning to risk rehashing the topic now.

"Probably take you longer to figure out the schedules and stops when you're not a regular rider than to just drive in and find parking."

"That may be, but I think I've figured out what I need now. I just hate that traffic downtown."

"All right, whatever." Todd turned to go. "I'll probably be a little late tonight. Faculty meeting."

"Okay." Sylvia pretended to sort through her email until she heard the garage door close. Then she picked up her purse and looked inside. The little zipped cosmetic bag containing the swabs looked innocuous enough. And the weather was in her favor. A pair of light gloves would not look out of place—and would conceal the rubber surgical gloves beneath. She donned both pairs of gloves and left for the park and ride.

Sylvia stood at the crowded bus stop, both pleased and disturbed that her research had paid off. Metro Route 554 satisfied her needs in every important way. Judging from the mob of people trying to board, it was a popular rush-hour commuter route, so popular a 554 would arrive at this stop every fifteen minutes for the next two hours. She tried to ignore her pangs of guilt at being so damned clever at figuring out how to turn a pathogen loose on unsuspecting victims.

The last of the crowd was boarding the bus. It was time to act now. She hesitated, knowing she could still walk away, and wondering if she should. But ... they'd taken all possible precautions, hadn't they? The pathogen wasn't that potent. No one would die. And if she failed to follow through, Horton would certainly cease to exist.

She palmed one of the sheathed swabs in her gloved hand and walked up to the bus. She stepped just inside, broke the seal, and trailed her hand along as many surfaces as possible as she approached the driver.

"Does this bus stop at Spring and Walnut?"

"No, ma'am. You'll want the 214 for that. There should be one coming right after the next 554."

"Thank you."

She stepped back off the bus and watched it close its door and drive off. Then she turned and hurried to the nearby trash receptacle and disposed of the open swab. Alone now, she sat on the bench and waited for the next 554.

So far, so good. She'd purposely asked about a stop she knew that bus didn't make so she would have an excuse to hop right back off. And the bus stop had emptied out for the moment, so when she repeated her little act in fifteen minutes, no one would recognize her and wonder what she was doing.

Yesterday afternoon, she'd weighed all the pros and cons of different approaches. At first, she'd thought she would stay on the bus and try to contaminate as many surfaces as possible during the ride. But she discarded that idea after playing it through in her mind. Too likely someone would notice her, plus there was the problem of disposal. She wouldn't want to slip the opened sheath back into her purse, but she also wouldn't want to be stuck holding it in her gloved hand for the duration of the ride.

Sylvia figured her chosen approach would maximize the number of people potentially exposed, minimize her own exposure, and allow her to dispose of the swabs without being noticed. She could also contaminate the bus benches when she was done, to aid the spread that much more. And because she'd chosen to carry out her plan during rush hour, all these people would be on their way to work, where they would in turn contaminate surfaces and other people in their offices and help do her work for her. It wasn't perfect, but it would probably get the job done.

Soon, people started arriving at the stop for the next 554. Sylvia realized she hadn't taken bus rider etiquette into account. Everyone appeared to assume she had simply arrived first for the bus and so they queued up behind her. She quickly tried to think if this affected her approach, and then decided it would be more awkward, but still possible, to do her fake inquiry of the bus driver. She took a deep breath to calm herself.

The 554 pulled up and opened its door. Sylvia palmed the next swab in her purse and stepped just inside the bus as she broke open the seal and trailed her gloved hand along the door, rail, and paypoint surfaces.

"Does this bus stop at Spring and Walnut?"

"No, ma'am. The 214 does, though. It's right behind me."

"Thanks."

She turned and struggled to get past the passengers jamming the door to board the bus. She made sure to touch a couple of people's backpacks as she went past them. Then she disposed of the swab in the trash on her way back to sit and wait on the bench.

Her stomach clenched as she noticed the bus had filled and two of the passengers were turned away.

They returned to the bench and sat on her left.

One of them grumbled, "They've got to add another bus to this route. Damned thing fills up all the time. I hate having to wait for the next one."

The other one nodded. "Me, too. Third time this week I had to wait for the next one."

The pair continued to complain to each other about lousy bus service as Sylvia fought off panic and tried to think of what to do next. They would expect her to get on the next bus. The last thing she needed was to get stuck actually taking the damned bus downtown and having to make her way back to her car here at the park and ride. But she'd look suspicious if she didn't.

Two buses was just going to have to be enough. She averted her face from the other two people, who, for the moment, were still engaged in their lively bitchfest about poor bus service, and palmed a third swab. She broke it open and rubbed it along as much of the bus bench surface as she dared, then stood, quickly dumped it in the trash can, and returned to her car.

CHAPTER 29

Emily Lewis was having a bad day. It had started from the moment she woke up that morning. Her stomach had been a little, well, off. Not quite bad enough to call in sick, but her morning coffee didn't seem to sit right, either.

She'd only recently started her job at the coffee shop, so she didn't have any sick leave built up. So, trooper that she was, she downed a little peppermint tea in hopes it would settle her stomach and headed in to work.

The coffee shop was a small, mom-and-pop sort of place near the University District, so her job responsibilities were broad and business was brisk. She greeted people as they came in, took them to their tables, and handed them their menus. She took orders from those who sat at the old-fashioned lunch counter and even handled all the customers' payments on their way out. Most days she felt she had to be in several places simultaneously. Most days, she had the energy to handle it, but not today.

About midway through the morning, she asked a coworker if the heat had been set too high. After receiving an odd look in response, she figured the problem was with her, not the thermostat. She stood at the counter and fanned herself with a menu as the last of the morning customers finished their food and paid their bills.

By mid-day, she started feeling much worse. Her throat rather suddenly became scratchy and painful. Swallowing felt like she was gargling with broken glass. Her nose started to itch and run. Emily hadn't planned for any of this, and so didn't have tissues handy. She had to keep dashing into the bathroom to get some

TP to blow her nose. And it just kept getting worse.

Finally, she asked a coworker to take over the counter crowd and her other duties so she could just handle the payments. Feeling too ill to stand, she pulled up a stool and slumped onto it. She mechanically took patrons' credit cards and cash, and hoped none of them were grossed out by the rashes that had developed on the backs of her hands.

Emily told herself to buck up, because in just a few more hours she could go home and go to bed. After all, she was a trooper. Troopers don't call in sick for just a little flu. They tough it out and earn their pay.

CHAPTER 30

Sylvia leaned back in her chair. She preferred the quiet and isolation of the lab, despite the necessary hassle of wearing her hazmat suit. The limbo-like environment fit well with her mood these days.

Several weeks had passed since she'd released the pathogen onto the buses, and there had been no dramatic announcement in the news to reflect it. This could mean one of two things. Either her plan had failed utterly, or it was working perfectly. She'd spent many hours in the interim wondering which was the case.

Unless and until the new disease became fairly widespread, it would likely be passed off by victims and health providers alike as just another vague flu-like illness. At least at first. At some point, if the disease spread adequately, it would become apparent it had its own fingerprint. At least, that was the plan.

Meanwhile, all they could do was wait. Jerry had withdrawn even further—if that was possible—and spent most of his time alone in his ResearchStation pod, doing some research or other. So she sat alone in the lab each day and wondered if she had managed to singlehandedly turn a new pathogen loose on the population. She made a wry face. What a great thing for the résumé.

Anxious to do something other than just sit and wait, Sylvia took a petri dish from the Pathosym's incubator and placed a sample of the pathogen on a glass microscope slide. She returned the dish to its slot and took the slide to the microscope. She clipped the slide onto the microscope's stage and turned on the light.

Idly she gazed through the lens at what, for better or worse, was a sort of progeny. It featured the chain-like structure of spheres typical of a staphylococcus, just like its ancestors, the original MRSA and the more recent, more deadly, MRSA-II. She watched as several strands wriggled across her field of vision.

But then something caught her eye that she didn't expect, and had never seen before. Two of the chains approached each other in a seemingly deliberate manner. Then they intertwined with each other. In a matter of moments, they completely merged. Bacteria normally reproduce by splitting, but these had merged together, clear as day.

She stared into the scope, barely breathing. What did it mean? After several minutes, she saw the merged pair redivide. She'd never seen bacteria behave in that way. Stranger still, the two newly divided bacteria moved differently than the others. They seemed somehow more ... purposeful.

Sylvia quickly grabbed a glass micropipette and guided it toward the new organisms as she watched through the scope's lens. She picked them up and deposited them in a fresh glass petri dish, which she then slid into one of the Pathosym's slots. She quickly tapped the control panel to order a complete analysis of these newly emerged specimens.

Something didn't sit right with her, but she couldn't put her finger on it. She decided to keep it to herself until the Pathosym reported its findings.

CHAPTER 31

Todd Barrett stood at the podium in front of his 1L Civil Procedure class and wondered what to do next. Granted, the students' energy and interest levels typically waned shortly into the spring semester, but this was ridiculous. The room was half-empty, and those who were present looked like zombies.

He decided to try a cold call to liven things up. "Mr. Anderson, what does the *Celotex* case tell us about the standard for summary judgment?"

His victim snapped to attention, or tried to. His mouth hung open like a fish out of water struggling to breathe. He cleared his throat. "Summary judgment?"

"Yes, you've heard of it, haven't you? Have you read today's cases?"

"Yes, Professor. I did." He drew the back of his hand across his forehead. "I just...can't quite remember ... I'm not feeling well today."

"Then why aren't you home in bed?"

"Afraid to miss class and get behind."

"I see. Volunteers? What's the standard?"

Not a single hand went up. Eyes darted in every direction except the front of the room, as if by doing so, they could make themselves invisible and therefore immune from the dreaded cold call.

Todd glanced at the time displayed on the wall in glowing green digits. Still a half hour left of class, but he was getting nowhere fast with this crew. "Are you *all* not feeling well today?"

Heads nodded silently.

"All right. Class dismissed. Get home to bed; get to Student

Health. Do what you need to do to get better—and try not to spread this around any more than you already have. Be ready to discuss today's cases next time class meets. Take care, everyone."

His students gathered up their things and shuffled out of the room before he could change his mind. As he watched them go, he realized this was the tail end of the flu season, and he'd never before had a class hit so hard by it. He shook his head and headed back to his office. He hoped if any of them visited him during his office hours that he didn't catch whatever they had.

CHAPTER 32

Anxious to see what the analysis revealed, Sylvia drew her chair close to the Pathosym console and tapped an icon to request the results. In a moment, the screen displayed the complete report.

She scrutinized the information, at first noting nothing surprising. The sample showed the organism remained pathogenic, yet sensitive to their antibiotic compound. The transmission mode remained the same, as did the profile of symptoms the organism would trigger in its victims.

The overall profile looked quite similar to that of the organism she and Jerry had designed. But that pairing and splitting behavior! It was too unusual not to reflect in some way. She had to be missing something.

Sylvia tapped another icon to display the two sets of results side by side with a delta analysis. She studied the report closely, looking for those data points where there was a difference between the two samples. Nothing. She continued down the list, finally encountering the only significant delta.

Tendency to mutate.

Her breath caught as she realized the significance of her finding and compared the contrasting measurements. The organism—as designed—demonstrated nearly no tendency to mutate. But the specimens that she saw spontaneously commingle and divide showed an extremely high tendency to mutate. Was this a one-off lab aberration—or could this have also occurred in the specimens she had released into the population?

Sylvia stood and stepped away from the Pathosym, as if putting physical distance between herself and the display would help her think clearly and calmly about what it had just told her. It didn't. Trembling, she pressed the button on her PortiComm through her hazmat suit, called Jerry, and asked him to come to the lab to discuss an important new development.

Two words ran through her mind as she waited for him.

What if?

Jerry arrived in the lab some minutes later after donning his protective gear and passing through the double doors.

"What is it?" He spoke in a clipped, cold tone, as if he didn't want to be in her presence a second longer than absolutely necessary.

"Jerry, we may have a problem."

He folded his arms. "With what?"

Sylvia explained what she'd seen under the microscope and what the Pathosym had told her in the delta analysis. Jerry just glared at her as she spoke.

"And what do you want me to do about it? That's the risk you take when you deliberately distribute a pathogen." He waved a hand toward the Pathosym. "Sure, we ran all the available tests, and our equipment is highly accurate. But given time, any organism can mutate. Looks like this one is capable of creating a version of itself that is exceptionally susceptible to mutation. I'd say all bets are off."

Feeling weak in the knees, Sylvia lowered herself into a chair. "Well, mutation doesn't *have* to be in the direction of increased virulence. No. It doesn't. And it doesn't *have* to be a major change. It could be more incremental. We deliberately used a mild pathogen in creating this organism." She looked up at Jerry, hoping he'd agree with her or say something to quell her gut-level fear of the worst possible scenario. She couldn't help but think now that she should have listened to her superstitious feelings before she'd taken those irrevocable steps to spread the disease.

"Yeah, we spliced a mild pathogen with an incredibly deadly one that killed an impressive number of people in a pretty short time before Denali came up with the cure. Come on, we need to let Phil know about this."

After explaining what they had just discovered, Sylvia looked almost physically ill, and Jerry sat with his arms folded and jaw clenched tight. As he grasped the implications of what they'd told him, Phil wished he'd never authorized the project in the first place. God knew what would happen now.

He pressed his fingers to his temples as the beginnings of a headache stirred inside his skull. "So, this particular strain mutated in the lab, right? We don't know for a fact that it's happened elsewhere?"

"No, we don't know that. I just happened to see what I saw under the microscope when I was doing some follow-up studies. I have no way to know if this has occurred outside the lab, or even if it's happened in any of the other colonies in the lab." Sylvia drew a trembling hand across her forehead as if she felt feverish.

Grimacing with sudden sharp pain, Phil leaned his head to one side to ease a spasming neck muscle. "So this could be a one-time thing or it could be a development of the gravest kind—we just don't know."

Sylvia nodded and stared into her lap.

Jerry spoke up. "I'm not sure what we can do with this information. It's not like we can recall what's been distributed. We don't even know yet how much or how far it's spread in the population."

Sylvia shot Jerry a vicious glare, then stood and faced Phil. "There *is* something we can do." She began to pace with increasing momentum as she spoke. "Let's say the organism *is* establishing itself and spreading out there. We engineered it to be highly contagious but to only cause a relatively mild illness. So the early … victims … are probably just self-treating for the symptoms. That's why we're not hearing about it yet. But knowing what we know now, that's dangerous."

She stopped pacing and faced Phil again. "We have to take whatever steps are necessary to make sure those who contract it are quarantined until the disease runs its course—or until they are cured, once the companion antibiotic is released. If people treat this like a mild illness, it's going to spread like … well, like we planned. Given the potential danger of it mutating to something deadly with no cure, we can't allow people to self-treat without quarantine."

"We can't do that."

"Why not, Phil? It's the only way!"

"For one thing, the disease hasn't yet been officially recognized, so how would you identify victims? And even once it is recognized, no one's going to submit to quarantine when all they have is a little flu-like illness, with maybe an upset stomach and a mild rash. That wouldn't even pass the laugh test. No medical professional would agree to that, and imagine the public's reaction. No way." He waved his hand to dismiss the crazy idea.

"Phil's right. The only way to convince the public or the medical profession that quarantine was appropriate would be to tell them what we found out today—and why it's a problem." Jerry didn't even look at Sylvia as he spoke.

"Which would mean admitting that we designed the organism and released it in the first place." Phil let out a slow breath. "I can't even count the ways that would bring the company down. Unacceptable. You'd better study the hell out of that mutation and try to figure out what we're really facing here." He stared down at his desktop. "It had better not mutate in the population—at least, not until we get a better grip on how to deal with it."

CHAPTER 33

Todd speared a mouthful of green beans onto his fork and held it up in the air. "What's with all the vegetables tonight? It's like you're trying to load me full of vitamins or something."

Sylvia cast him a sharp glance. "What do you mean? We usually have vegetables with dinner."

"But beans and broccoli, too, tonight? They're good, it's just that we usually have one, not two."

"You don't have to eat them if you don't want to." She stabbed at her beans with more vigor than seemed warranted.

Since the topic of vegetables inspired wrath for some reason, Todd decided to change the subject. "I had to end a class early today. Never had to do that before."

Sylvia sawed at her steak with single-minded fury. "Why?"

"Well, half the class was out, and the rest were unprepared when I called on them because they were sick."

She forgot about her steak and stared at him. "Sick? Sick how?"

"I didn't get into the intimate details with them, but they all raised their hands when I asked if they were sick. They looked pretty pale and out of it." He chuckled. "Of course, the first-years tend to flag about this time in the second semester anyway."

"Your *whole class* is sick? How many is that?" She dropped her fork and leaned forward.

"Oh, about sixty, I'd say." He speared a piece of broccoli. "Why are you so interested?"

"It's really irresponsible of them to come to class and expose everyone to their disease." She eyed him closely. "Did you get near any of them?"

Todd put down his silverware and raised his hands, palms out. "Whoa, chill, will you? This happens every year. It's just worse than usual this time. The law school's great about sending mixed messages. On the one hand, Student Health sends out notices about staying home and not spreading germs. But at the same time, there's constant competition, and there's plenty of pressure from that. The students are afraid to miss something and somehow disadvantage themselves later on exams."

"But they're endangering their own health—and the health of others!"

"Will you calm down? It's probably some little bug that's going around. It happens. I'm sure it's the kind of thing people always complain about. Sick enough to be miserable, but not sick enough for a doctor to do anything about it anyway. Just have to let it run its course, drink fluids, and all that crap." He smiled. "It's not that big a deal. Really. My class was just hit a little harder than usual this year. I'm sorry I mentioned it."

Sylvia pushed away her plate, her dinner unfinished. "I wish people would be more responsible about their health. Those kids should do the right thing—and if they won't, the school or Student Health should step in. That's how epidemics happen, because people don't have the brains to stay home when they're sick and contagious." She got up and stormed from the room.

Todd stared at his plateful of green vegetables and grilled steak. He wondered why such a simple remark about his day had set Sylvia off like that. After all, it was just some stupid little bug going around. Just like every year.

"Aren't you hungry?"

Distracted from his thoughts, Phil glanced up at Livvie. She sat across from him at the dinner table, her soft brown eyes fixed on him with concern.

"Oh, sorry. It's just … well, something difficult arose today at the office."

"What is it? Maybe it would help to talk about it."

He shook his head. "No, it's pretty complicated. Actually, I'd like to go try to think through it for a while, if you don't mind."

"Well, okay, if you don't think I can help."

"I appreciate it. Maybe once I get my own arms around it a bit more." He rose and headed down the hall to his home office.

Phil switched on the light and closed the door. Then he went over to his desk and dropped down into his high-backed swivel chair. He sat slumped, staring at nothing and wondering how the hell he was going to get through this. He'd been right. His only qualification for this job was his last name. Nothing more.

And now this. Not bad enough he lacked the skills to keep the boat afloat, but in trying to save the company, he'd authorized the very project that might just torpedo that boat to oblivion. He should have known better than to try to beat that fucker Tremaine at his own game. It wasn't the Horton way, and there was a reason for that. Horton only knew how to play the game with the utmost integrity. It had been a pillar of BigPharma for years doing business that way.

Then that upstart had to change the game. Would the industry ever be the same? Was there really any point in trying to save Horton, if that's how the game would have to be played from now on?

Phil shook his head. That was a question for another day. Right now, he had to focus on the immediate problem: had they released a pathogen that might mutate into something even worse than the deadly MRSA-II? Maybe, maybe not. But if it *was* capable, what could he do about it?

He grimaced and smacked his forehead with his fist. Oh, it had been such a perfect plan, hadn't it? What a great way to build market share. Too bad the disease's own characteristics made for the ultimate potential disaster if the organism ever decided to mutate into something more dangerous.

Sylvia was almost certainly right in presuming it was out there spreading, because people were likely doing their usual thing of going to work sick rather than using their sick days—and thereby spreading it even more. And because of its generic symptoms, it hadn't yet achieved the visibility necessary to identify it as a specific disease so they could warn people.

Phil decided the risk was too great to hide his head in the sand and hope the organism mutated in a benign way—or not at all. He decided on a two-pronged strategy. On the one hand, he'd have Sylvia and Jerry study the mutation potential in the lab and work on a drug to address the organism's most likely mutant version. On the other hand, he'd move ahead now with the needed preparations for producing the drug they'd already developed, rather than waiting for the disease to spread enough to be specifically identified. This meant the overall market would be diminished to some degree in releasing sooner than the original plan, but that was how it had to be.

It was the right thing to do.

CHAPTER 34

Arms folded, Jerry leaned back against the wall outside the entry to the lab as he came to a decision. He'd let Sylvia run alone with the project since their green-light meeting with Phil. She was the one all ready to go, to jump headlong into something that was not the Horton way. He couldn't believe Phil had proposed the plan in the first place. Must be testament to just how badly the company was floundering in the wake of Denali.

And he'd never dreamed Sylvia would find it so easy to set aside basic ethics. Maybe she wasn't the person he'd imagined her to be.

But now, Phil didn't seem willing or able to grasp the magnitude of the potential disaster that loomed; he surely hadn't demonstrated the necessary courage or leadership to address it. Sylvia had taken it as her personal responsibility to try to find the solution, and was working herself to death in that lab. Jerry decided it was time he pitched in to solve the problem, even if he hadn't supported the foolish decisions that had led to it.

He aligned his right eye with the retinal scanner to unlock the outer door. Once inside the vestibule, he changed into his hazmat suit, then took a moment to prepare what he'd say to Sylvia. Hoping she wouldn't reject his offer to help, he unlocked the second door with another retinal scan and entered the lab.

Back hunched, Sylvia sat rooted before the Pathosym. She glanced at him, then turned back to her work.

"What are you doing here?" Her voice was cold, dismissive.

"We have a lot of work to do. I think Phil's in denial of how serious this could be. The organism may never mutate, or it might do so in a harmless way, true enough. But we have to prepare for the worst-case scenario." He stepped forward and took a seat next to her in front of the Pathosym.

"I guess I'm in no position to turn down help, given the stakes. But I thought you wanted no part of this. You've made that clear for weeks." She eyed him closely. "I haven't even seen you around, you've made yourself so scarce."

Jerry swiveled his chair to face her. "You're right. I believe this project should never have happened. Horton should never have chased Denali like this. But that's a beef I should take up with Phil at some point, not you. It's done now, and given the potential implications, I can't stand by and not try to figure out a way to minimize the risk to the public."

Sylvia turned away and spoke softly. "I've thought about it almost nonstop since I saw the mutation, and I know I should never have agreed to do what I did. I guess I let my competitive side get the better of me, and it was stupid … and unethical. Should never have done it." She faced him again. Her eyes gleamed with unshed tears. "Thanks, Jerry. I'm really glad you're here."

Uncomfortable with the turn of conversation and with his resurging feelings for Sylvia, Jerry cleared his throat and returned to the business at hand. "What do you have so far?"

Sylvia took his cue and scrolled through the most recent test results on the Pathosym's screen, highlighting the key data points as she did so. "Thing is, I don't know what triggered the behavior I saw that led to the mutation-prone strain, and so it's hard to give odds on whether that would happen out in the field. You know, it was really weird to see. It almost looked like intentional mating behavior."

"Mating behavior?"

"Yes. I know that sounds ridiculous. One-celled bacteria do not mate—they divide to reproduce. But those two bacteria seemed to deliberately approach each other. Then they merged and combined their genetic material. When they redivided, the resulting pair contained different genomes than before the … mating."

Jerry couldn't buy her interpretation. She seemed to be attributing to a bacteria some level of intelligence that couldn't possibly exist. "Well, purposeful or not, it happened and the result was a far more mutagenic version of the pathogen."

"That's right. So it comes down to this: how can we get it to mutate in the lab as it actually would out in the field? That's crucial, but I don't know how we do that with any certainty in the result."

"Yeah, that's exactly what we need. We get that, and we can likely develop the needed antibiotic with the Pathosym." Jerry thought for a moment. "I think the only thing we can do is set up an accelerated breeding program, and split it into several populations so we cover the different conditions it may encounter—well, as best we can."

"Tell me."

"Okay, you have the strain that created itself. There's one population. The other starting population consists of the strain we developed. We can breed generations of each of these populations, and if mutations develop, those would form additional populations to analyze. While we're at it, we should set up populations of each version to expose to our drug, just in case it happens to affect the tendency to mutate. It's a study we'd want to conduct anyway— might as well do it in parallel with the rest."

Sylvia remained silent for several moments as she digested his idea. "I like it. It covers the possibilities the best we can with what we know at this point."

"We can always adjust or add another strain to the study if something arises along the way."

Sylvia smiled. "Then let's get busy."

TURNING THE CORNER

CHAPTER 35

Dan Tremaine finished reading the article on his FloaTouch display and slammed his hand on his desk.

"Damn Horton to hell!"

Vince flinched at the outburst as he stepped inside Dan's office for their scheduled meeting. "What is it?"

"Horton took a page from our book. No fucking way did they come up with Spectrocillin that fast. They must have engineered the pathogen first."

Vince sat down. "Oh, that. What's the disease been named? Generalized Infection Syndrome, or GIS? Yeah, I saw the story, too. Well, if they did, it was a good strategy. People don't want to lose two weeks of work with a pain-in-the-ass illness when they can take some pills and stop it in its tracks."

"Spreads like wildfire, too. Like nothing we've seen before. Good thing its mortality rate is zilch. Can you imagine if it were more dangerous?"

Vince shook his head. "I don't even want to think about that. If they did engineer it, they took a real risk making it as contagious as it is."

"They should be raking it in on this one. Demand is sky-high. Their problem will be keeping up the needed production levels." Dan paused, a wicked smile spreading across his face. "On the other hand, maybe they're actually *losing* money on Spectrocillin. They have so much old infrastructure to maintain over there— the extra load on their systems could accelerate maintenance costs." He laughed. "Hell, no way can they compete with Lucracillin on profit margin, thanks to our dear president Coleridge and the federal government."

"I don't see how anyone could beat Lucracillin's profit margin. Even if their infrastructure were more modern, you just can't beat zero production costs."

"True enough. So now, Vince, let's discuss our next project."

Phil Horton gazed across his desk at his CFO, Chuck Seaforth. Only a few months ago, he would have dreaded a visit from Chuck. Not that he was a natural bearer of bad tidings, but there were simply no other tidings to bear at Horton back then. He leaned back in his chair and clasped his hands behind his head.

"So, Chuck, what's the status?"

"Phil, you've done it. A year ago, I wouldn't have given Horton odds to remain in business much longer. The financials were that bad. This new drug, this Spectrocillin ..." He shook his head in amazement. "It's really done it. Horton is not only no longer on life support—it's actually thriving."

Phil leaned forward with his elbows on his desk. "Where are we in relation to Denali?"

"Well, we're thriving, but our profits aren't stratospheric like theirs. We're solidly Number Two in BigPharma now, but they are still way in the lead. That said, we're very strong. Horton would do quite well just staying in this position indefinitely."

Phil considered his CFO's remarks for a moment. He'd love to destroy Denali in the marketplace. He hated everything Dan Tremaine stood for and how he ran his company. But ... to do that, he'd have to stoop to Tremaine's ethical level.

And he would not do that. At least, not again. Every day he thought about the possibility of GIS—*their* GIS—going rogue out there in the population. But, so far there had been no sign of that happening. Could it be that Sylvia's panic over its mutagenic potential was overblown? He could only hope so as she and Jerry worked hard to try to determine what conditions might trigger mutation—and what sort of mutation would be most likely. So far, they had no concrete results.

Chuck looked at him quizzically. "Were we done?"

"Oh, I'm sorry. Something crossed my mind and distracted me. What were you saying?"

"Oh, I was done. I was just asking if you had questions and

you drifted off on me with a really intense look on your face."
He smiled. "Must be some weighty matter. Care to discuss it?"

Phil waved his hand. "Oh, no. Nothing we need to talk
about. No, I have no questions. Thanks for the update."

After Chuck left the room, Phil closed his door, set his
PortiComm to "Do Not Disturb" so all calls would go straight
to voice mail, then sat quietly, alone with his thoughts. Maybe
the danger of mutation had passed. Maybe he was worrying for
nothing at this point.

After all, everything had gone exactly to plan.

CHAPTER 36

*"*Sylvia?" Todd checked the living room, then wandered down the hall. *Where is she?* He continued on into the kitchen, and noticed the sliding door to the deck was partly open. He went over to the screen and looked outside.

Dressed in shorts and a T-shirt, Sylvia reclined in a deck chair, a glass of iced tea on the small table next to her. Todd remained silent as he took in the scene and tried to decide what to say. It was a beautiful Sunday afternoon and she had been working so hard lately. She'd seemed terribly stressed for some weeks now, but hadn't confided in him.

And no wonder. The last time she'd tried to confide in him, he bit her head off and put her on the defensive. Ever since, there had been that chilly layer of distance between them. He didn't like it. They'd only gotten married late last summer, and it wasn't right to have a rift like that so soon—or ever. He slid open the screen door and went outside.

"Sylvia?"

She turned toward him, the mid-spring sun glinting off her dark sunglasses. "Yes?"

He slid the other deck chair beside hers and sat down on it. "We should talk. I don't like the distance between us."

She turned away from him and gazed straight out over the back yard, her expression neutralized by her sunglasses. "Well, you put it there."

He looked down at his hands. "Well, perhaps I was a bit … harsh. You've seemed pretty stressed lately. What's going on?"

"Well, in some ways, things are going extremely well. But in others …" She sighed. "The pathogen we designed is out there causing GIS, and the Spectrocillin that cures it is readily available to anyone who needs it. It works perfectly, and there is strong demand."

Todd wondered exactly how a pathogen manufactured in the lab got *out there*. Not really wanting to know the answer, he restrained himself from asking that question and let her talk.

"Phil says it's pulled Horton Drugs back off the brink of bankruptcy and is actually turning the finances around quite nicely."

"Sounds like all should be well, then."

She looked down into her lap and hesitated before responding in a subdued voice. "There is one problem. Well, *maybe* there is a problem. We're not entirely sure. Right now, the pathogen is behaving exactly as we intended, but I did some additional testing after I saw something strange in the lab. There is a possibility a strain may develop that is much more prone to mutation than the one we designed."

Todd felt his stomach clench. He was no scientist, but this sort of thing was exactly what had worried him when she had first let him in on the project. He struggled to ask his question without sounding judgmental, so she would be more likely to open up. "Prone to mutate how?"

"That's the problem. We don't know yet. We don't know *if* it will mutate, let alone how it might and what that might … mean."

Todd feared he knew the answer to his next question, but he had to ask it anyway. "Do you have some sort of a plan?"

"I wish we did. How do you plan for something that may or may not happen, and if it does, you don't know what effect it will have?"

"Well, what if it *does* mutate in a dangerous way and Horton could have warned people ahead of time?"

She lowered her glasses and glared at him. "Always the lawyer, aren't you?"

"Well, doesn't it sound like a massive and highly visible lawsuit waiting to happen? It doesn't take a bar license or a spectacular imagination to envision how it would play out."

"Maybe *you* should go talk to Phil, then. Perhaps he'll listen to you. He sure hasn't listened to me on this. I tried to suggest that we somehow get the word out that people who contract GIS be quarantined while they're contagious. It was a nonstarter with him." She let out a brief, sarcastic laugh. "Our own design is working against us. GIS may be highly contagious, but Phil's right on one point. No one's going to take quarantine orders seriously for an illness that, untreated, just makes you miserable for a couple of weeks and then is gone. But I think a quarantine protocol is the only way we could stave off an epidemic in the event it mutates in a dangerous way."

"Well, even knowing what you do know about the potential danger, can't Horton Drugs make some sort of announcement that would help convince the medical profession to recommend quarantine?"

She shook her head. "Nope. Even if we could convince the public health powers-that-be that quarantine was appropriate, Phil will never agree to it. Properly done, quarantine would stop the spread of GIS and eradicate it from the population. That would kill off the flow of profits from Spectrocillin. And any such announcement would raise questions about the origin of the GIS pathogen—something Phil doesn't want exposed, for obvious reasons."

"Do you—does he—realize what position he's putting Horton in if this does go south? It would bring the company down. The civil suits would bleed it dry … and there might well also be criminal charges brought. And even if it doesn't mutate, I still think Horton would likely face legal consequences for designing GIS in the first place—I can see why he wouldn't want that to get out." His mouth went dry at the possibilities, and the thought of Sylvia being implicated along with Horton.

She held her hands out as if to push his words away. "Look, I only saw something that made me want to do further investigation. It is far from certain that there is any danger at all. You're running off into the worst-case scenario already."

"That's what any good lawyer should do—especially given the magnitude of the risk this could represent on so many levels. Sylvia, I can already see the scenario playing out." He put his hand on her shoulder. "And I don't want you involved in it. Please.

Promise me if you do find it's likely to mutate, you'll get the hell out of Horton Drugs and not actively promote a cover-up. You just can't participate in anything like that, not if people could die and if Horton knows it and still won't do what's necessary to prevent it."

Sylvia lowered her head and rubbed at her temples as she took in his advice. "I wish I'd never agreed to help design the damned thing. I just got caught up in trying to save the company, and thinking I could do it without any serious risk. Really. We were careful in the genes we selected for combination, and if it doesn't mutate, it's all good." She sounded on the verge of tears.

Todd felt terrible for her, but he had to make one more point clear while they were having a productive conversation instead of an argument. "Well, even if it doesn't mutate ... think about how the story would sound if it ever came out. Horton created a pathogen so it could create and sell the cure. Even if no one died, that isn't the height of ethical behavior. I can't imagine that would not entail consequences on its own merits."

Sylvia's face flushed red as she tried to defend herself. "We're nearly certain Denali already did it—and with a far more dangerous pathogen."

He held up a hand. "I know. All the kids are doing it, so that makes it right. Horton is still making people sick so it can sell its product."

She sat up on the edge of her deck chair and shook an angry finger in his face. "Welcome to the real world. Don't you realize the companies that make the anti-cholesterol meds own the big fast-food companies—under shell names, of course? And don't you think they have a hand in the ingredients to make sure cholesterol is a big enough problem to make a market for their drug? You might as well indict the whole industry, Todd."

"All right, all right. Let's not argue about that aspect now. But seriously, if this has the potential to turn dangerous, you cannot be part of the cover-up. Do you understand?"

She slumped back down and sighed. Then she spoke in a quiet voice. "Yes. I do. I promise. If I confirm we have a problem, and Horton won't take meaningful protective steps, I'll resign."

Todd reached over and took her in his arms. "That's it. If

you do that, you'd have a decent defense and I could find a colleague to protect you from the legal shitstorm that would surely hit." He kissed her cheek. "I love you and I just want to protect you. I don't want to see you take the fall for Horton's desperate acts."

CHAPTER 37

"Oh God, no." Sylvia glanced again at the Pathosym display. She prayed she had read it wrong.

But she hadn't.

Jerry was at the other end of the lab, emptying the autoclave of a batch of freshly sterilized petri dishes. "What's the matter?"

"Finally, we have a material change in a colony, a descendant of the mating pair that we've exposed to Spectrocillin." She felt sick to her stomach as she turned to face him. "Jerry, it's become resistant."

He paled, then rushed over and sat beside her at the Pathosym. "What's its disease profile?"

"I haven't run that yet. I just found the resistant colony. I'll set up the test right now."

Jerry spoke softly, almost to himself. "It may be resistant, but if it still only causes a mild illness, it won't be the end of the world."

"Let's hope. It worries me that this colony descended from the organisms that exhibited the mating behavior." As she spoke, she transferred a sample of the mutant bacteria to a fresh petri dish. "Of course, that is the line of organisms we suspected would be most likely to mutate, so I suppose that's to be expected."

Jerry's forehead crinkled as he considered her comment. "I'm still not certain that any mutation we get in the lab would realistically represent what would happen in the field. There are just so many more variables outside the lab that we can't predict or mirror." He watched her place the sample in the Pathosym slot and start the analysis. "Best we can do, though."

"I know. I can't get that out of my head, either. I'm at a

loss for what else we could do to emulate field conditions any better than we have, though." She drummed her fingers on the desktop as she stared at the empty display.

Jerry gently rested his gloved hand on hers. "The Pathosym is fast, but staring at it like that won't make it any faster."

"Yeah, I suppose not." Not sure how to read Jerry's touch, she placed both her hands in her lap as they waited for the analysis to complete.

They sat together in tense silence as the Pathosym did its work. Neither moved, and despite Jerry's remark, neither of them could help but stare at the Pathosym's display while they waited. Sylvia couldn't have focused on anything else anyway.

After about twenty minutes that seemed like as many hours, the Pathosym signaled with a soft chime that the analysis was complete and ready for review. Sylvia noticed a slight tremble in her hand as she touched the icon to request the results.

Jerry let out a breath. "Here we go."

The display filled with a list of parameters describing the mutation's anticipated disease profile. Sylvia took a deep breath and, despite having been so anxious to see the results, now had to force herself to look. She'd dreaded this day ever since she witnessed the mating behavior, and her recent discussion with Todd had only given her more reason to fear what she might be about to learn.

Jerry clapped his hands to his hazmat-suited head. "I don't know how it could possibly be worse."

Sylvia felt weak and hollow when she finished reading the analysis. Jerry was right. The mutant version was capable of spreading at least as—and possibly more—readily than their original GIS pathogen. It would cause a disease that would make MRSA-II look mild. It, too, would attack and eat flesh—but far faster. Worse, because of its gastric component, it would attack the digestive tract from the inside at the same time as it ate flesh from the outside. And it would do it all so quickly that even the most effective drug would have an extremely brief window in which to be administered.

This new pathogen would be vicious. And unforgiving. And it was resistant to Spectrocillin.

A thought occurred to her. A thought so sinister and foreign that at first she tried to brush it aside. "This is going to sound insane, but I'm going to say it anyway. I think it did it on purpose."

"What?"

She turned to Jerry. "Remember when this all started, what I saw? Those two that joined together. They *approached* each other. I remember thinking at the time that the behavior seemed almost ... sentient. They very deliberately approached each other, then joined. That enabled them to redistribute the genes in a different way—a way that allowed them to mutate and become resistant to the drug. And they merged the most dangerous features of their genetic ancestors: the easy spread and gastric effects on the one hand, and the MRSA-type effects on the other."

"No, it can't be. Bacteria aren't sentient. This is just genetics and mutation coming together in a bad way. That's all."

"Jerry, you did not see what I saw. It wasn't random."

He waved a hand at her. "I can't accept that. I *can* accept that we have a major problem on our hands here."

"I know what I saw."

Jerry looked as shaken as if he'd just witnessed a fatal accident. *As well he has*, she thought. He finally found his voice. "We have to talk to Phil. Now."

CHAPTER 38

"What is it you want to talk about?" Phil stared at Sylvia and Jerry. They both looked like hell—pale, haggard, and agitated. This couldn't be good. He shifted in his chair as he waited for one of them to speak.

Jerry looked at Sylvia. "You saw it first. Go ahead."

Sylvia squared her shoulders, took a deep breath, and explained their findings and what the Pathosym had reported. "We wanted to let you know immediately, given the obvious implications."

His throat constricted as he turned to Jerry. "You're of the same opinion, I take it?"

"Yes. She was the first to spot it, but we both reviewed the Pathosym analysis. It's solid. The worst possible combination of features."

Phil leaned back in his chair and rubbed his jaw as he searched for any possible defects in their analysis. "So this was the strain that descended from the pair you saw that merged, then split again, right?"

"Yes." Sylvia's lips formed a straight, tight line. "Well, you know, I don't want to downplay your hard work, but don't you think this is the least likely scenario to be concerned about? I mean, that pairing was such an odd thing to happen in the first place, it may have been induced by something specific to the lab environment." He leaned forward to make his point. "You know how hard it is to fully emulate field conditions. So it's highly likely that would never occur outside the lab. The base GIS strain is behaving just fine, no mutation, no resistance to the drug, right?"

Sylvia sat rigid in her chair. "I've—we've— thought about that as well, and you may be right, but given the Pathosym results, I don't think we dare take the chance. If something like this *did* develop in the field, it would explode into an epidemic faster than anything we've ever seen before, with a disease that will eat flesh and digestive tracts so aggressively that even if we had a drug to combat it, it likely couldn't even be administered in time. How can you take a chance on that?"

Phil stood in an attempt to show his authority and take control of the situation. "You both know as well as I do what the stakes are here. You cannot guarantee this would happen in the field. I *can* guarantee that if we did anything proactive about this, it would involve admitting that we designed a pathogen, and you can be sure Horton Drugs would be destroyed. In no uncertain terms, and in a short amount of time." He walked over to his window and turned his back to them. "I can't allow that. Horton is just getting back on its feet. I can't blow that over a scenario that is merely *possible.*"

Jerry jumped up and nearly knocked over his chair. "Phil, you're not hearing us. If this thing hits, it'll be like nothing anyone's ever seen before. I don't even want to estimate the death toll."

Phil turned to face them again. "Test it against Denali's Lucracillin. Mutation or not, this organism descended partly from MRSA-II. If that works, then we have a different situation entirely."

Jerry sat back down and ran his hand through his hair. "That's a good idea. I was so upset with the Pathosym analysis, I didn't think of that. We can do that right away."

"I have something to say first." Sylvia stared straight ahead and gripped her chair's arms so tightly her knuckles whitened.

"No, not now." Jerry grabbed her upper arm and she shook him off.

"No, *now.* If you don't believe me, fine. But I'm not keeping this to myself any longer." She glared at Jerry, then turned to Phil. "I have a theory based on what I saw. I'm the only one who saw it, and Jerry is having trouble believing what I have to say about it."

Phil scowled as he took in the strange vibe between Jerry

and Sylvia. He'd never seen her like this.

"What is it?"

"It's about the source of the strain that mutated into the one we're reporting on today. It is my opinion, based on what I personally observed, that the originating pair displayed intentional behavior when they joined together, then later split. It was a deliberate—and I think sentient—act." She sat back in her chair and folded her arms across her chest.

"You've got to be kidding." Phil fought off an urge to roll his eyes. Had this come from anyone other than Sylvia, he would have laughed outright.

"I saw it myself. Neither of you did. I believe it was deliberate, and it was done to shift the genetic composition to a more mutagenic form. This enabled the organism to later become resistant to Spectrocillin and to merge the most dangerous features of its predecessors together into the deadliest bacteria ever."

"You're convinced of this."

"I am."

"Well, even if you were right—and I must say I'm surprised to hear something like this from you— what difference does it make? It happened in the lab, where maybe there was some condition that triggered it that would not occur out in the field. Test for sensitivity to Lucracillin and we go from there. I'm not destroying Horton Drugs over speculation." He shook his head. "Sentient bacteria. Let me know what Lucracillin does to it. And Sylvia, maybe you need some rest."

Sylvia set her jaw and shot him an angry glare before storming from the room. Jerry shrugged his shoulders and left without another word.

Phil dropped into his chair and laid his head on his desk. The sentient bacteria theory was clearly the product of an overworked mind, but what if they were right about its ability to mutate and the nature of the mutation they could expect in the field? He didn't want to even try to picture a world with a pathogen like that on the loose.

CHAPTER 39

Hoping for the best but expecting the worst, Jerry sat in what had become his regular spot beside Sylvia in front of the Pathosym. He watched as she raised her hand to the control panel, then put it back in her lap without tapping any of the icons.

"I'm afraid to look."

"So am I, but we have to know if the strain is sensitive to Denali's drug." He sighed. "Or not."

"I know."

Before Sylvia could protest, he reached over and tapped the control panel to request the answer from the Pathosym. "Sorry. I just have to get this over with."

Sylvia gasped when the results displayed.

Jerry thought he'd braced himself for the worst, but he still felt like an unseen hand had just delivered a vicious blow to his gut when he saw the report.

"Oh, God. Instead of killing it, the Lucracillin *stimulates* its growth. I've never seen anything like this."

Sylvia turned to him, her eyes wide and all color drained from her face. "You know what this means, don't you? It *designed* itself to create the maximum possible damage."

"I don't believe it's done any of this intentionally, but if that were possible, it couldn't have done it any better." Jerry tore his gaze away from the Pathosym as the greater implications of the test results struck him. "This strain would produce symptoms to mimic MRSA-II—only worse—and so doctors would almost certainly prescribe Lucracillin to combat it, at least initially."

She slapped the counter. "Yeah, and that's just what it wants.

It would trick them into giving it exactly what it needs to strengthen and multiply like mad. And spread like nothing we've ever seen."

Jerry didn't accept her irrational attribution of sentience to the damned thing, but the end result was the same, whether by design or by chance. The mutant strain was perfectly set up to create a public health disaster of epic proportion.

"We've got to figure out a way to head this thing off."

"Without a drug that's effective against it, I can't think of anything we can do other than order quarantine for victims of the version we—I—put out there." She stared into her lap. "But we've already been down that road with Phil."

"Maybe he'll be more open to it now that we know Lucracillin's effect. Or not. Beyond the fallout for Horton Drugs, a call for quarantine might cause a widespread panic throughout the nation and beyond." He thought for a moment. "You know, quarantining GIS victims wouldn't be enough anyway. What if someone comes down with *this* version in the field, not the original GIS? It would be diagnosed as MRSA-II or close enough, and the obvious choice would be to administer Lucracillin. And the thing would be off to the races."

"My God, you're right. What are we going to do?"

"We'd damned well better find what it *is* sensitive to and develop a drug. And faster than we've ever done it before."

Sylvia's head sagged. "I don't think it's possible."

He grabbed her shoulder and shook it. "It had *better* be possible. And we'd better do it. We'll run that Pathosym day and night until we do."

CHAPTER 40

Vince Calhoun sat alone at a small table in the spacious Denali solarium. He'd staked out a spot near one of the tall, full, living ficus trees and relaxed in the gentle sunlight that streamed through the ceiling and walls made from adjustable-opacity WindoWall glass. Most of the other Denali researchers and scientists kept themselves in their ResearchStation pods to avoid distractions, but he found the openness of the solarium helped him think more creatively. With his PortiComm, he could access the Internet and his own files just as easily as in his own pod or office. He drew a deep breath and stretched his shoulders.

Today, however, he found himself with little to do. Despite Dan's demands, he hadn't yet started on a new designer pathogen. Something in his gut told him it would be better to wait, just to be sure their MRSA-II pathogen didn't do anything unexpected out there in the population—even though Lucracillin was performing admirably to cure the victims. Rather than argue with Dan, he'd just hunkered down and made busy work for himself lately.

Vince decided to take a little stroll through the Internet and see what was going on in the world. He activated his PortiComm and the FloaTouch display appeared before him. He idly flipped through his favorite news sites with no particular destination in mind. Nothing notable going on. Just the usual Wall Street gyrations, corporate scandals, celebrity dramas, and the like. More dull tedium. Maybe he should leave early and go for a run or something.

Then a story caught his eye. At first, it looked like just another one of those Denali-bashing stories. Muckraking journalists loved to throw barbs at the successful kid on the block. He read further. A doctor in Vermont claimed he had a MRSA-II patient—a young waitress named Emily Lewis—who died despite receiving Lucracillin in the proper dosage just after the initial onset of the disease. If the story was accurate, this was the first case where the drug hadn't been completely effective.

Not wanting to risk being overheard, he shut down his PortiComm and went straight to Dan's office to tell him what he'd just read.

"I'm worried. If this story is accurate, then a resistant MRSA-II strain may have developed. If so, we need to get in front of it, and fast."

Dan scowled. "Understood. Drop your work on the new pathogen for now and get hold of that doctor. See if you can get a sample that you can culture and work with."

"Will do." Rather than savoring a feeling of righteous I-told-you-so vindication, Vince found himself trying to shake off the unsettling sense of dread that had just swept over him.

"Paging Dr. Riley ... paging Dr. Riley."

Tom Riley groaned. He still had several critical patients to check on, and he needed a break two hours ago. He turned away from the door to his next patient's room and strode down the hall toward the nurses' station.

"Call for me?"

The nurse wore a puzzled look. "Yes, it's an outside call. A Vince Calhoun from Denali Labs. He says it's urgent."

"Why are they calling me? I don't have time for drug salesmen." The hospital was supposed to have people to handle the endless parade of BigPharma salesmen. He sure as hell didn't have the time—or desire—to listen to the song and dance.

"I had the same thought at first, and I told him so. In no uncertain terms. But he insisted that wasn't why he was calling, that it was about a specific patient."

"All right. I hope he isn't trying to pull a fast one to get around the normal procedure. I wouldn't put it past any of those guys. Pushy bastards. Patch it into my PortiComm, please."

Tom pressed a button to accept the call. "Hello, this is Dr. Riley."

"Doctor, thank you for taking my call. My name is Vince Calhoun, and I'm the lead research scientist here at Denali. I'm calling about what might be a very urgent matter."

"Mr. Calhoun, I'm very busy today, so get to the point. What is it?"

"I read in the news that you had a patient, an Emily Lewis, who apparently had contracted MRSA-II, but who died despite having Lucracillin appropriately administered."

Tom wondered why someone from the manufacturer would be calling. Probably to see if there was any way he'd screwed up in administering the drug—so they could avoid any possible liability. That's how these outfits worked. Granted, they came out with some really useful drugs, but if anything went wrong, their lawyers were the first to figure out some way to absolve them of any responsibility. They left the doctor exposed to the malpractice claim every time.

"Yes, I did. I administered the drug precisely as per the label instructions. I've been having excellent results with it in my other patients. But this time, it just didn't work." He sighed. "If anything, her disease process appeared to accelerate. She didn't last the night."

"Really? This is the first I've heard of the drug failing at all, let alone of any incident involving an acceleration in the pathology. I'd like to investigate this further and try to determine what made this case different. Would it be possible for you to send samples to me for culture and testing?"

"Well, of course I'd have to check with the next of kin before I could promise anything like that. The body is still in the morgue downstairs, so I'd still have ready access if they agree to it."

"Please, Dr. Riley. I really hope you'll be able to get those samples to me. I want to understand what happened here and see if a resistant strain has developed that we should be aware of. It goes without saying that we don't want to ignore that possibility with a disease as dangerous as MRSA-II."

"True enough. I remember all too well how it was before the drug became available. One hundred percent mortality.

Lucracillin has saved many lives, just here at this hospital." He gazed into the distance as he pictured his patient. "This case, though. It really was worse than anything I'd seen before. I sure hope there was some underlying weakness in the patient, because if the bacteria has mutated ... well, let's just hope it hasn't. I'll check with the next of kin right away. They're pretty upset as you can imagine, so it might be a couple of days before you hear back from me."

"Thank you. I really appreciate it."

Tom took Calhoun's contact information and ended the call. Funny, he'd never had a drug company demonstrate that much seemingly genuine concern over the performance of its product. In this case, he was glad they did.

He didn't want to think about what it would be like if they couldn't depend on Denali's silver bullet for MRSA-II infections. He would be sure to get permission from the next of kin, no matter how much coaxing he had to do.

CHAPTER 41

Connie Morgan braked to a stop and opened the bus door. She watched as the passengers boarded. It never ceased to amaze her how zombie-like they all looked as they got on the morning bus to work and school. They all shuffled in and waved their pay cards at the reader like the walking dead. Come to think of it, they didn't look much better by the end of the day. She smirked, confident none of them would even notice how she was looking at them.

Unfortunately, she didn't feel so terrific herself this morning. She'd have loved to have stayed home in bed, but was running short of sick days. Just a few weeks ago, she'd been hit with some weird bug. Knocked her on her ass for days. She'd finally called a friend to commiserate about it, and her friend told her there was some great drug that would fix her right up.

So she'd gone to the nearest walk-in clinic and asked for whatever would take care of that awful bug. They gave her an injection and a vial of pills and sent her on her way. She went home and took the medicine as directed. And damned if she wasn't feeling just fine by the very next day—this after days of lying in bed, barely strong enough to get a glass of water every few hours. Amazing stuff.

Connie wondered if she was having a relapse now, after such a miraculous turnaround. She made a mental note to get herself over to the clinic again after her shift. She didn't have time now, and hoped she would make it through the day before she really started dragging badly again.

A particularly stupid-looking passenger shoved a five-dollar bill in her face and asked for change for the machine.

She took the bill in her hand, raised it up and pointed to the sign at the front of the bus. "See that? We don't take currency anymore. Don't you have a pass card like everyone else? You just wave it at the sensor over here and it deducts the fare from your account. We stopped taking currency last year." She handed the bill back to the passenger, who just stood there looking perplexed.

She waved her hand in exasperation. "All right. Go ahead and get on. But make sure you get a pass card before you try to get on the bus home tonight, all right?" Connie didn't feel like arguing. Breathing took too much effort as it was, her stomach felt a bit sour, and she was developing a really intense itch on her back beneath her bus driver's uniform.

This was going to be a long day.

CHAPTER 42

"Thanks for meeting with me, Phil. I really need to talk to you alone." Jerry shifted in his chair. He didn't want to say what he had to say, but he knew it needed to be done.

"Sure, Jerry. What is it?"

"We've done some more testing and the results are, well, disturbing. The mutant strain is resistant to Denali's Lucracillin."

"I was hoping we'd catch a break there. I suppose it shouldn't be that surprising, though. Their drug was designed specifically to affect the MRSA-II bacteria. It was probably so specific to it that it couldn't possibly work on anything else. Well, we'll just have to—"

"Phil." Jerry's mouth went dry as cotton as he prepared to deliver the worst part. "There's more."

Phil frowned. "What?"

"Lucracillin isn't just ineffective on the mutant strain. It actually *accelerates* its growth and pathological effects."

Phil paled. "Accelerates?"

"Yeah. Its growth rate skyrockets—and its effects intensify in tandem. The Pathosym models indicate the mutant strain would kill a victim within hours instead of days. And it would retain its extremely contagious nature."

Phil put a hand to his forehead and closed his eyes a moment. "Oh, that's just great."

"It's even worse than that. Think about it. Patients will present looking like they're infected with MRSA-II. Given that disease's history and pathology, doctors will quickly administer—"

Phil's eyes widened, then his hands dropped to his desk and lay there, impotent. "Lucracillin. Oh, Jesus. It's a perfect storm."

"Yes, it is. Sylvia's gotten it in her head that the organism is sentient, that it planned exactly this scenario. I don't believe that, of course, but if it were ... it couldn't possibly have designed its mutant version better for maximum spread and impact."

Phil sat back in his chair and ran a hand over his mouth. Tiny beads of sweat appeared at his hairline. "My God."

"We've already started analysis to design a drug to combat it. We're moving as quickly as we can on that, of course."

"Of course. But how do we know this very same mutation will happen in the population? I still don't think we can know that for certain."

"That's true. We could be chasing a phantom. But dare we take the chance? I don't know what else we can do."

"No, you're right to proceed as you are. I know Sylvia was pushing to call for quarantine. I still don't want to go that route. There would be no way to even suggest that without tipping our hand as to why—and as to the fact that we designed the damned thing in the first place." He stared down at his desk. "No. We do that and Horton Drugs might as well shut down for all the scandal and liability that will ensue."

"We talked about that some more. Quarantine still could help prevent some of these cases, but mainly for those who contracted GIS or MRSA-II first and *then* the mutant version. That wouldn't necessarily be the most likely scenario. The more likely scenario is someone contracting the mutant version that mimics MRSA-II, and then that person is treated with Lucracillin—the logical choice given the initial symptoms."

Phil wiped the sweat from his hairline with a trembling hand. "We'd better hope you and Sylvia can design a drug in time."

"Yes." Jerry shifted in his seat again. "Phil, I want to say something else. I hope you understand where this is coming from."

"What is it?"

"Well, you and I have both been here at Horton a long time. I'm not part of the Horton family, but I almost feel that way. I cut my teeth here and have been here my entire professional life. I just want to say ..." He took a deep breath, then looked Phil in the eye. "I just want to say, I wish this hadn't happened, and I don't think Horton Drugs would have taken this route in the past. I really wish we hadn't compromised Horton standards to try to keep up with Denali. It just doesn't feel right."

Phil suddenly stood and stomped over to his window. He put his fists on his hips and turned his back to Jerry before answering. "And what would you have done in my place, Jerry? I understand you've been here longer than about anyone, but it's a different reality these days. If we didn't play Denali's game, do you think we would even now be sitting here talking about it? My CFO would say not. Do you have any idea how close to corporate oblivion we were before we released the GIS bacteria—and the Spectracillin to cure it?"

Jerry flinched at the sudden verbal assault. He'd figured Phil would have shared at least some of the same feelings, but he seemed to accept that keeping the corporation alive, no matter the cost, was the primary goal. Maybe he was less of a Horton than Jerry.

"Sorry. Maybe I shouldn't have said anything."

"Maybe not. Maybe it isn't your place to criticize what I've had to do to save this company. You think it was easy for me to cast aside Horton tradition?" He waved his hand in a dismissive gesture without turning to face Jerry. "Maybe you'd best get back to the lab. Before it's too late."

Jerry stood. "Yes, sir. I'll do that." He'd given his total loyalty to Horton Drugs all his professional life. Perhaps it didn't deserve it.

But for now, he had to work to make sure that if the worst possible thing happened, they were ready.

CHAPTER 43

After Jerry left, Phil felt his knees threaten to buckle beneath him, so he returned to his desk and sat. He leaned back in his chair and noticed how tension had driven his shoulders up toward his ears. He took a deep breath and made a conscious—albeit unsuccessful—effort to try to relax them.

He hadn't worked directly with Jerry before now, but he knew of his excellent reputation at Horton. He didn't deserve to be treated the way he'd just treated him. Jerry was right and he'd struck a nerve. Phil knew perfectly well there was no way Horton Drugs would ever have stooped to designing a pathogen of any kind just so it could create a revenue stream.

And was it really worth it? What was he saving if he had to sacrifice Horton Drugs' long-held ethical standards to do it? They were no better than Denali now. And what was worse, they may have unwittingly unleashed on the public a monster far worse than MRSA-II—and without a cure.

Phil leaned his elbows on his desk and held his face in his hands. He had to think through what he'd learned today, had to come up with a solution. And he had no one he could confide in. Not for the first time, he wished he'd never taken over as CEO. He'd never even been remotely interested in the position, but he'd felt obligated to take it and do his best. And now he'd made a good, solid mess of it.

He pressed a button on his PortiComm and called home. "Livvie? I've, uh, got some work to do tonight. I'll be here late. Don't hold dinner for me."

He stared toward the window. "I think I'm going to be quite late … yes, it's something major. I wouldn't wait up if I were you."

He hung up and decided he needed a change of scenery.

Phil settled into a booth in the back of the Harlow Lounge, a little place between his office and home where he sometimes stopped for a beer at the end of the day. He'd hoped the change in setting might spark some much-needed inspiration, and figured because the Harlow was a quiet and cozy sort of place, that he'd be left alone to think. He hadn't expected the place to be nearly devoid of other customers.

He signaled the waiter and ordered an IPA and some onion rings. As he waited for his order, he glanced around the room and wondered if any designer bacteria lurked on any of the surfaces—or if any of the staff or what few customers there were harbored the mutant version of the pathogen. He ran a napkin over the table in front of him, and tried not to think about how much he'd like to douse the entire booth in rubbing alcohol.

His order arrived in record time. The waiter set the glass of beer and plate of onion rings before him, then asked him if he needed anything else.

"No, this is fine, thank you." He pointed toward the main section of the lounge. "Where is everyone? I realize it's a weeknight, but it's so empty."

"Been a ghost town here for the past several weeks now. People are staying home more because of that GIS bug that's been going around." He sighed. "This keeps up, old man Harlow said he may have to close up until things settle down."

"I'm really sorry to hear that."

"Thanks. Well, enjoy your food. Let me know if you need anything else and I'll get it to you right away. Personalized service, seeing as you're almost the only one here tonight." The waiter forced a smile, then headed back to the kitchen area.

If this place was losing business because of the GIS outbreak, imagine what would happen if the mutant strain started spreading. Phil took a swallow of the IPA, then set it down and stared at it, watching the bubbles form, rise, then destroy themselves. He picked up an onion ring and began to concentrate on his dilemma.

CHAPTER 44

Beads of sweat lined Connie Morgan's hairline as she checked her watch for the thousandth time. She was just about to pull her bus into the terminal for the day, and there was still time to get over to the walk-in clinic on her way home.

She'd never felt so terrible in all her life. The day hadn't started out all that great, and as the hours wore on, she felt sicker and weaker, like some really vicious bug had a grip on her. What's more, there was that painful itching under her uniform that she hadn't been able to shake all day. Unable to really get at it, she'd been rubbing her back against her driver's seat. At first she'd worried the passengers might notice. By the end of the day, she didn't care about the passengers at all, and only wanted to get out of her uniform and scratch and claw at her skin directly. Even if it bled.

With a sigh, she pulled into the parking spot reserved for her bus. She wiped her forehead with the back of her sleeve, tottered out the door and locked it. She hurried on unsteady legs to her car, tossed her purse onto the seat and got in. She leaned her head on the steering wheel for a moment as she fought off a wave of dizziness. She hoped it didn't get any worse before she could see a doctor.

She started the car, eased out of the parking lot, then turned onto the road behind the bus terminal. She was grateful that it wasn't yet dark and the way to the clinic was a pretty straight shot from the terminal. She didn't trust herself to do battle with heavy traffic or a long drive. Driving the bus around all day had taken everything she had.

The honk of a horn startled her as she realized she had begun drifting into the oncoming lane. She gripped the wheel tighter and tried to focus all her attention on driving. She wanted desperately to scratch her back, and nearly pulled over to do it, but she didn't dare delay herself.

Teeth gritted and shoulders hunched, Connie felt a small wave of relief when she spotted the Urgent Care sign up on the next block. Surely they would give her something that would make her feel better. Whatever she got last time she was sick sure worked like a charm. She turned into the driveway and took the first open parking spot.

Connie grabbed her purse, got out of the car and locked it. A sudden blackness encroached at the sides of her vision. She leaned against her car for support, resting her head against the door frame. She struggled to muster the strength to get herself in the door of the clinic. That was all she needed to do. They would take care of her and make this misery stop.

After a few moments, she felt stable enough to try again. She headed for the clinic door, opened it, and made her way to the reception desk.

"Hi, I need to see a doctor—"

The receptionist gave her a startled look, stood, and pressed a button on her desk. "Stay right there."

The door beside the reception desk opened. Two white-uniformed men wearing surgical masks and gloves came out and approached her.

"Come with us, ma'am," said the one on her left.

Before she could protest or even react, they each took one of her arms. They half carried her into the treatment area, even though the waiting room was full of other patients.

The next thing she knew, she was seated on a gurney in an examination area, the curtain drawn around her. One of the men left, and the one who remained informed her he was one of the doctor's assistants. Moments later, the doctor arrived, also wearing a surgical mask and gloves.

He nodded to the assistant and said, "Vitals."

The assistant helped her to recline on the gurney, then placed a cuff around one arm and a sensor in her ear. "BP 90 over 60, temperature 104."

"CBC and blood chemistries, then set up an IV." The doctor

stepped closer and looked at her sharply as the assistant left to get the needed items. "When did this start, what else are you experiencing?"

"This morning. Been getting worse all day. I feel feverish and just sick all over. Everything hurts. My stomach's kind of upset, too." Connie licked her dry, cracked lips. "And the itching. On my back. It's been horrible all day, worse now."

"Let's take a look at that." The doctor helped her to sit up so she could remove her uniform shirt. He handed her a paper gown, which she clasped to her chest as he stepped around to take a look at her back. The doctor gasped.

"What is it?"

Without responding to her, the doctor pressed a button on the wall beside the gurney and shouted, "IsoStat kit for Room 4, NOW!"

The doctor positioned himself as far as possible from her within the curtained-off area that surrounded them. Remaining on the gurney, she put on the paper gown in a clumsy and ineffectual attempt to feel less vulnerable.

"What's going on?"

"Your back. It looks to me like a MRSA-II infection. That'll have to be confirmed, of course, but we can't take a chance that it is. It's highly contagious, so we're going to put you in a portable isolation unit right away. And if it is MRSA-II, you'll need to be transferred to a full-service hospital. We can't keep you here for the necessary treatment."

"Well, it can't be that. It must just be some rash. I feel feverish, so it must just be a breakout of some sort from that."

The look on his face silenced her. "I wish it were only that … Ms., um … They didn't take your information at the front desk, did they?"

"No, I must look like hell. They took one look at me and just whisked me in here before I could say much of anything. It's Morgan. Connie Morgan. Look, I just had some other sort of bug recently. I got some medicine for it and got better really fast. Maybe it's just a relapse of that."

"Ms. Morgan, I'm sorry, but I've seen a number of MRSA-II cases and I know what it looks like. There is a relatively new drug—Lucracillin—that is extremely effective in treating it. But the disease remains contagious even while the drug regimen is administered, so we have to take precautions. A hospital stay is required, I'm afraid. We're not set up to admit patients to stay here."

Connie scratched her forearm, then noticed a new lesion there. It was already a couple of inches across and was oozing a mix of yellowish serum and blood. Heart pounding, she thrust it toward the doctor. "Is this what's on my back, too?"

"Yes, it is. How long has that one been there?"

"I just now noticed it, and it's so big already."

The doctor crept a little closer for a better view, then stepped back, nearly tripping on himself. "Hurry up with that IsoStat!"

"What's the matter?"

"I've never seen it move that fast. I saw it enlarge just in the moment I took to look at it."

Connie looked down at her forearms. Not only was it visibly larger in just minutes, but now there was a lesion on her other forearm that hadn't been there even moments ago. "Oh my God, what *is* this?" She held her arms out away from her, repulsed. Her arms, her back—it was spreading so fast!

The assistant arrived with a metal cart that held what looked like a stack of clear plastic sheeting. "Lie down flat for a moment, please. This won't take a minute. He draped the plastic over her and the gurney.

"What are you doing?" She lay down, then started to flail at the plastic, feeling like she would suffocate with it pressing her down.

"Hang on just a minute."

The assistant flipped a switch, then the plastic rose and took shape as the air baffles in its walls inflated. In a matter of moments, the plastic sheeting formed an enclosure around her and the gurney.

"What's happening? What are you doing?"

The doctor approached. "Try not to let it upset you. It's just a disposable, portable enclosure that sets up a barrier to keep the disease from spreading. It protects us and the other patients— though we will need to disinfect ourselves and the area to eliminate whatever contamination has already occurred."

"*Contamination?* You can't be serious."

"I'm quite serious. It's a precaution we have to take because this looks so much like MRSA-II. We'll run labs right away to determine that." He nodded at the assistant.

The assistant approached the plastic enclosure from the side and inserted his gloved hands and the blood draw supplies through the double barrier port nearest her arm. He quickly drew the blood and removed the samples through the port. After wiping the outside of the tubes with a disinfectant, he left the room.

"We'll have the results in only a few minutes," said the doctor as he stared down at her through the plastic. "Do you feel any itching or pain anywhere else right now?"

Connie thought for a moment, then realized her legs itched as well. She sat up inside her enclosure and hiked up the lower edges of her pant legs. "Oh my God."

Lesions like the ones on her arms covered her calves. She looked again at her forearms. The lesions had continued to spread even in the short time since she first noticed them.

The doctor scowled at her calves. "You say you only started feeling ill this morning?"

Moments later, the assistant reappeared. "Looks like MRSA-II. The lab wants to run another test on the sample to be 100% sure, though."

"We'll have to assume it's MRSA-II for now in the interest of time. It's spreading incredibly fast on her. Arrange for transportation to the hospital, and in the meantime, let's get her started on Lucracillin."

"Right." The assistant hurried from the room.

The doctor turned to Connie. "Don't worry. Lucracillin is amazing. You'll see." He smiled. "I've never seen a drug act so quickly and so effectively. Try to stay calm."

"How could this have happened? I felt perfectly fine just yesterday, but I barely made it through work today before coming here."

The doctor frowned. "You were at work all day today? Where do you work?"

"I drive a muni bus—downtown and back."

The assistant returned with a small vial and a syringe on a metal tray. "They're arranging for transportation now. Shouldn't be too long."

"Good. Give her 2 cc's. When you're done, we need to get Triage working on this. She drives a bus, drove it all day today. That bus requires decontamination before it's used again, and all of today's passengers are at risk of exposure. Need to see what can be done about that once we get her stable and on her way."

"Got it." The assistant drew the dose into the syringe, then reached through the double barrier port to inject the drug into her vein. He removed the syringe and sealed it in plastic for disposal. "I'll go talk to Triage to get things moving." He left Connie and the doctor alone.

The doctor stepped over and gazed down at her. "It'll take several doses to complete the treatment regimen, but I've found that even the first dose makes a world of difference pretty quickly for patients."

Connie lay on the gurney and hoped he was right. So far, she didn't feel one bit better. If anything ... suddenly her back burned like nothing she'd ever felt before. Searing pain attacked her arms and legs, starting from where the lesions had been, and radiating out to consume her limbs entirely. She screamed as the burning spread across her chest and belly, then up her neck to her face.

The assistant ran back into the room, and he and the doctor stared down at her through the plastic barrier.

"Her skin! The lesions are consuming her right before our eyes! What can we do?"

The doctor shook his head and shifted from foot to foot. "I don't know—I've never seen MRSA-II move this fast. Never."

Connie looked up at them, trying to form a question, but the pain was too great for her to do any-thing but scream. Then her eyes began to burn and the room darkened. She felt herself screaming, but could no longer hear it. Her heart hammered in her chest, then slowed, then she no longer felt it at all.

Like a wave receding on the beach, the pain released its grip on her.

CHAPTER 45

Vince Calhoun sat in his lab dressed in a full hazmat suit. Usually he felt confined by the suit and so he minimized his physical time in the lab. Today, his work consumed him so completely, he forgot his discomfort.

The victim's family had been cooperative, and so Dr. Riley had been able to get him a sample shortly after their phone conversation. Vince had allowed the sample to grow in a culture for several days so he'd have a sufficient quantity to conduct whatever tests he might need. Anxious to get started, he removed the petri dish containing the culture from his specially modified Pathosym's incubation slot and set it on the counter before him.

He placed a sample of the culture in each of two fresh petri dishes. Then he placed a dose of Lucracillin in one of the petri dishes, and inserted each dish into a slot in the Pathosym. One sample would be tested to determine the nature of pathogen and the disease it produced, while the other would be tested for sensitivity to the drug.

As he waited for the Pathosym to do its work, he congratulated himself on the modifications he had made to the baseline Pathosym III model. Those changes enabled this particular machine to complete its tests in half the time required by the unmodified model. All the other BigPharma companies undoubtedly had Pathosyms—but none were as fast as his.

The Pathosym sounded a soft chime to indicate the profile testing was complete. He scowled as he reviewed the results on the screen. The pathogen caused a disease that looked very similar to MRSA-II on the surface, but was indeed far more virulent and dangerous. It attacked a victim on the outside with the familiar lesions—*and* from the inside, with lesions forming inside the intestinal tract and spreading to the vital organs when the GI tract eventually perforated.

The results correlated with the disease's course as Dr. Riley had observed it in his patient. There was apparently nothing uniquely vulnerable about his patient—the disease was really that vicious.

The remainder of the analysis showed the pathogen was of more recent origin than MRSA-II. Indeed, it appeared to combine portions of MRSA-II's genetic sequence with some other highly contagious bacteria that produced much milder symptoms. It also had a significant propensity to mutate. He wondered if Denali's MRSA-II had mutated in the population—or if some other mechanism had spawned this particular pathogen.

The Pathosym chimed to indicate the culture and sensitivity results were ready. He glanced at them and flinched. Not only was the bacteria resistant to Lucracillin, it actually *thrived* on it.

He activated his PortiComm with a voice command and called Dan to explain what he'd found.

"You know what this means. This thing looks so much like MRSA-II that the first-line treatment will be Lucracillin. Precisely the thing that will put it into overdrive."

Dan let out a low whistle. "That's quite the profile. I'd much rather we'd developed this ourselves so we could have had total control over the release of a companion drug." He paused, then began to speak at a manic pace. "You know, if this thing spreads and word gets out, there'll be panic in the streets. We'd better be ready with the cure, ASAP. We'll be able to name our price on this one. Given that profile, no one would dare quibble, even if the government has to step in to subsidize treatment. This is great news. Thanks for letting me know."

Vince ended the call and sat for a moment in amazement. Dan was a marketing genius, no doubt about it. Who else could take news like that and spin it into a new business opportunity without batting an eye?

SUPERBUG

CHAPTER 46

President Coleridge sat in the Oval Office, staring at the wall of flat-panel screens and wishing he wasn't experiencing a nasty case of déjà vu. Even though the peak of the crisis had passed months ago, the MRSA-II outbreak remained a fresh and painful memory. They'd solved the problem before too many people died, but not without massive expenditures. And not without risk. Damned good thing Denali Labs had managed to find the cure so quickly, before the epidemic got out of hand and created global implications.

Now there was some other bug out there—far more deadly and far more contagious than even MRSA-II. Just out of the blue, it seemed, reports started coming in of people being stricken with a disease that looked a lot like MRSA-II initially, but did not respond to Lucracillin. Like MRSA-II, it attacked and ate flesh. But unlike MRSA-II, it attacked from the inside as well as the outside, and so had been named Acute Somatic Autolysis, or ASA. Thousands had died from ASA in a matter of weeks, and the Homeland had been thrown into hysteria.

The stock market had plummeted to levels not seen this century. Some days, the volatility was so great that the automatic trading curbs kicked in. He wondered about those curbs, and whether they helped stabilize the markets—or whether they just fueled more panic by their mere presence. The economic pundits had all taken great pains to avoid the words *free fall*, but any idiot could see what was happening. Other nations' markets had taken significant hits as well, prompting a worldwide ban on incoming flights from the U.S. Flights to the U.S. weren't banned, but nearly all had been cancelled because no one in their right mind wanted to travel into what was quickly becoming viewed as a hot zone.

Citizens were frightened, and justifiably so. They were hiding in their homes, not going to work, not shopping. Schools had shuttered their doors until further notice. Hospitals and anyone associated with health care were begging for a cure. *Now.*

A knock sounded on his door. "Come in."

John Humphrey, his secretary of Health and Human Services, plodded in and took a seat. His normally neat hair was disheveled and dark circles lay beneath his eyes. "Good afternoon, Mr. President. I have the latest—"

"Never mind the stats, John. I've heard enough just watching the news."

Humphrey closed his mouth and waited with a worn, defeated look on his face.

"I'm sure it's going to be expensive, but I think we need to do what we did to address the MRSA-II outbreak."

"The competition?"

"Perhaps. I think we should check in with Denali first. They came up with Lucracillin so quickly last time, maybe we can just deal with them solely. Eliminates a few complexities, if we can go that route."

"Sounds good."

President Coleridge activated his PortiComm and called Dan Tremaine at Denali.

"Dan, I'm calling about the ASA outbreak. I have John Humphrey here with me. I'm going to put the call on speaker." He touched a button on his PortiComm. "I'll get right to the point. ASA is similar enough to MRSA-II that I wondered if you were already working on something for it."

"It is similar, but as you know, it's resistant to Lucracillin. Turns out Lucracillin actually stimulates it. We are working on developing a drug specific to ASA, but don't have anything quite yet."

"I see. Well, the crisis calls for bold action, so I'm prepared to address it as we did with the MRSA-II outbreak. Since you don't have anything ready yet, I'm going to hedge our bets and call Horton in on this, too. Same deal as last time."

"Certainly, Mr. President. I have every confidence we will come up with something shortly, and I will let you know the minute we do."

"Thank you, Dan. Good luck."

He ended the call and let his eyes drift back to the flat panels on the wall. "Damn. Wish they'd already had something ready or nearly so. I'll have to get Horton on board again." He took a closer look at Humphrey. "You look terrible, John. I'll make the call. You should go home and get a little rest."

"Thank you, Mr. President. I appreciate it. I haven't been home all week."

Phil Horton slumped at his desk, punishing himself by watching the nonstop media coverage of the ASA epidemic on his FloaTouch display. He'd made the wrong bet—a deadly bet. He'd been a fool to believe that the mutation Sylvia and Jerry found in the lab wouldn't eventually arise in the population. Now a whole lot of people were dying and even if he came clean about Horton's role, it wouldn't stop the deadly march of what was easily the most dangerous pathogen ever.

He wished he had encouraging news from Sylvia and Jerry, but despite his constant checking, there had been no news to be had. Despite all their hard work and the Pathosym's technological prowess, the solution remained elusive. He shuddered to think of how long it would have taken to find the cure the old-fashioned way. Didn't matter. People were still dying at a horrifying rate while they used the fastest technology possible to solve the problem.

His PortiComm rang, jarring him out of his miserable ruminations. He took a sharp breath and his heart began to pound when he glanced at the caller ID. The president was calling.

He cleared his throat and pressed the button to take the call. "Hello, Phil Horton speaking."

"This is President Coleridge. I'm calling about the ASA epidemic. We have to act fast on this, and I'm proposing another competition between Horton and Denali to find the cure ASAP. Same terms as before. Whoever finds it first will receive full manufacturing and distribution support and financing from the government. I presume you're willing to participate again?"

"Certainly, sir."

"Good. I contacted Tremaine at Denali moments ago. Good luck. Please let me know immediately if you develop something we can use."

Phil pressed the button to end the call, leaned back in his chair and wiped the sweat from his upper lip. Nothing like a little more pressure. They were already working as hard as they could on the cure, with nothing yet to show for it. Now the conditions were in place for Denali to beat them again, gain yet another insanely lucrative contract with the government, and kill off Horton once and for all.

The irony was not lost on him.

CHAPTER 47

Sylvia slammed her gloved fist down on the lab counter. Several petri dishes clattered, and one nearly fell to the floor. "Damn it!" Her voice sounded close to breaking.

Jerry hurried toward her from the other end of the lab, where he was filling the autoclave. "What's the matter?"

"The Pathosym still hasn't been able to come up with a compound that so much as slows this fucking bug down." She clenched and unclenched her gloved fists in impotent rage. "I'm scared we won't find anything … ever. The fucking thing's out there, spreading … and killing. It's going to shift from epidemic to pandemic before long, I just know it. And then—"

Jerry sat in the chair next to hers and put a hand on her shoulder to try to comfort her. Sylvia had made an egregious and deadly mistake in agreeing to release the pathogen, yet it pained him to see how hard she was working to counteract the consequences, and how much guilt she had taken on in the process. He wished they could turn back the clock, for all their sakes. Then everything would be different. "We'll find it. We will."

She glared at him, her eyes red with unshed tears. "When? How many more people will die while we're trying? How many have already died? I've lost track, locked up here in the lab." She turned away and lowered her voice. "You were right. I wish I'd listened to you. I wish Phil had listened to you. Look what this has caused. People are dying horrible deaths. Everything's going to hell. People are afraid to go out, to go to work. The stock market is tanking. No travel in and out of the country. My God, the economy could actually collapse if this doesn't end soon."

Jerry wished he could assure her she was exaggerating,

that it wasn't all that bad. But it was. The only good thing about the general panic and publicity was the recognition that ASA was a different disease than MRSA-II. Doctors were less likely to administer Lucracillin without first making damned sure which disease they were treating. That was some small comfort; at least that helped minimize the number of Lucracillin-fueled ASA cases.

"They're using those disposable IsoStat isolation pods when a patient presents with anything remotely resembling either ASA or MRSA-II. That's got to be helping slow the spread."

"It's not enough and you know it."

"Well, I know, but until we have a cure—"

"No. It's *not* enough. Don't forget, even the original version of the GIS bacteria that we designed is capable of mutation. And still no one is being quarantined when they contract GIS. Who knows how much that's adding to the spread of the mutant strain?"

Jerry nodded and let out a long breath. "You're right. We can't know how much of a factor that is, but it is another potential mechanism for the spread of ASA—or some other mutant strain."

"Yeah. No matter how you look at it, this thing's got the upper hand, and we're sitting here with all our fancy equipment and nothing to stem the tide."

"It should never have come to this."

"What do you think I've been saying? I wish to God I could take back that day I planted the fucking thing on those buses. I can never, ever forgive myself for being so stupid, so smug that we'd designed something that couldn't possibly get out of hand. Stupid!" She smacked herself on the side of her head, the sound dampened by her hazmat suit.

He grabbed the back of her chair and swiveled it to make her face him.

"No, Sylvia. That's not what I mean. I'm thinking back to twenty, thirty years ago and probably even before that. We set ourselves up for this. Back then, antibiotics were miracle drugs, the answer to everything. They were prescribed at the drop of a hat for even minor infections. They were prescribed for daily, routine use in farm animals to get better yields for meat, eggs, milk—which humans in turn consumed. So what

did bacteria do? They did what they needed to do to survive—
they developed resistance. And we developed more and better
antibiotics. It became an arms race, pure and simple."

"Survival of the fittest."

"That's right. Now look at us, as an industry. We had to develop
the technology to create ultra-specific drugs to combat more and
more resistant bacteria. And we largely succeeded. But then
we couldn't leave that alone. Ego and greed got involved. I'll
bet MRSA-II wasn't the first pathogen that Denali engineered, and it
won't be the last. Where will it end?"

"It's going to end in total annihilation if we can't figure
out a cure for this one. That much I do know." Sylvia squared her
shoulders and turned to the Pathosym. "We've got to figure this
out."

CHAPTER 48

"That's it for today. Remember, your mock motions for summary judgment are due next week." Todd Barrett stepped back from the podium and wished he could just leave for the day. He wasn't up to dealing with the usual group of hypercompetitive students that swarmed him after class to ask questions about the assignment.

"Professor Barrett, what format do we use?" asked a thin, anxious-looking young woman with thick glasses.

"I posted a sample on the course Intranet, Ms. Gallagher."

"Oh right, thanks! I forgot." She smiled, blushed, and retreated.

"Professor Barrett, I'm still having some trouble understanding the requirements for personal jurisdiction."

"That's a longer discussion, Mr. Carmichael. Please, make an appointment to come to my office to discuss that one."

"Sure, thanks."

Todd fielded various questions—large and small—from the students for several minutes, then held up his hand. "Sorry, I need to get back to my office right now. Email me the short questions, and make appointments for the larger discussions, please."

Todd let out a sigh of relief as the students dispersed and fled to their next classes. Normally, he didn't mind fielding their post-class questions. But not today. He'd felt fine when he left home in the morning, but in just the last few hours, he'd started to feel incredibly tired and somewhat feverish. He headed upstairs to his office to hide out until his afternoon class.

He shut his door and hoped that would give any visitors the

impression he was out or busy with a private matter, so he would have some peace and quiet for a while. He stepped around his desk, dropped down into his chair, and noted the time. His next class didn't start for a couple of hours. Time enough to do something he hadn't done in years. He decided to take a nap at his desk. Surely he would feel a little better after that.

Todd rested his head on his desk, then scratched the itch that had begun to spread across his shoulder. He fell asleep in just a few minutes.

Sylvia pulled into her garage, shut off the engine, and rested her head on the steering wheel for a moment. Another day, another failed attempt to find the cure. Another day, and that many more people will have died.

She was not surprised to see Todd's car already there. Late yet again, she'd have to pull something out of the freezer to come up with some semblance of dinner, though cooking was about the last thing on her mind right now. She probably should have let Todd know she'd be this late. He could have gotten them some takeout.

She headed inside and flicked on the kitchen lights. Her shoulders slumped when she glanced at the counter. No sign of any surprise takeout or other progress toward dinner. She sighed and set her purse down on a chair.

"Todd?"

She stepped into the darkened living room and turned on the lights. Todd lay on the couch, apparently asleep. She walked over to him.

"Todd? Sorry I'm so late again."

He opened his eyes and regarded her with a somewhat dazed expression. "Oh, hi." He grunted. "Must have fallen asleep." He tried to sit up, then slumped back down.

Sylvia didn't like his color at all. She reached out and touched his forehead. "You're burning up. When did this start?"

He licked his lips as if they were parched and painful. "Oh, a few hours ago. I was fine this morning, then just suddenly went downhill. I tried to sleep it off for a while in my office, then felt so bad I had to cancel my last class and come home."

He struggled to raise himself up, then leaned against the back of the couch. Once steady, he vigorously scratched his shoulders, then his forearms, through his shirt.

A chill ran up Sylvia's back as she watched. "Why are you scratching?"

He shot her a sarcastic look. "Because it itches, of course."

"Itches? How bad?"

"Pretty bad, and it's been getting worse. At first it was just on this one side. Now it seems to have traveled some."

Before he could object, she unbuttoned his shirt and helped him out of it.

"Oh my God."

"What?"

She stood up and took a step back, nearly stumbling against the coffee table. "We have to get you to the hospital. Right now. Put your shirt back on. I need to sanitize my hands."

"Don't you think you're overreacting a little?" Heart pounding, she took a few more steps back, her hands extended away from her. "It's my fault. Oh, God."

He made a wobbly attempt at standing. "What is your prob—"

"Stay there! Put your shirt on and sit down. You're highly contagious."

He sat, a perplexed look on his pale face. "What is going on?"

"I didn't tell you the latest development. We've been working like hell to find the cure. The GIS pathogen we engineered has mutated. It starts out looking like MRSA-II, but it's much more … serious. Lucracillin only makes it worse."

"*What?* It mutated? To that ASA bug—and you think I have it?" Todd turned even whiter.

"I hope I'm wrong, believe me I do, but knowing what I know, we can't take a chance. I've got to get you to the hospital right away. And … you'll need to be quarantined."

Todd pushed himself back into the couch as if to distance himself from her words. "Quarantined? Are you serious? I was around students the better part of the day."

"Can't do anything about that right now, but you have what looks to me like an active infection. Put your shirt back on. We need to try to contaminate as little as we can here and in the car."

Sylvia went upstairs, got an old blanket and returned to the living room to find Todd with his shirt on and his arms folded across his chest.

"Come on, hurry." She spread open the blanket and stepped toward him.

"This is—"

"Don't argue with me. We have to go. Now."

Sylvia barely heard Todd's protestations through the adrenaline haze that consumed her. She bundled him up in the blanket and managed to hustle him into her car. Then she ran back into the house to get a bottle of rubbing alcohol and a roll of paper towels. She returned to the car, where she had him wipe down all his exposed skin with the alcohol and she did the same. It was primitive, but she had to do *something*. The Pathosym's profiling had revealed that the bacteria was highly contagious, but mostly through direct touch with another victim or a contaminated surface touched by a victim. Fortunately, it appeared to be less likely to spread through airborne transmission. At least she hoped the Pathosym was right on that point.

She started the car and gunned it into reverse. The tires squealed as she shifted into Drive and set out for the hospital.

"Can't we just—"

"Shush. I have to concentrate." She bolted past one car and nearly clipped another in her haste.

"Look out!" Todd's arms shot out in front of him in a defensive gesture as she pushed her luck on a late yellow light.

CHAPTER 49

Sylvia pulled up to the Emergency entrance and skidded to a stop. "Stay put. I'll be back as fast as I can."

The terrified expression on Todd's face tore at her heart, but there was no time to lose. She turned and headed for the entrance, determined to do what needed to be done before she lost her nerve.

She hurried to the triage desk. "My husband's outside. I think he may have ASA."

The nurse nodded and pressed a button. "Possible ASA case waiting outside." She looked up at Sylvia. "Someone will be right with you, ma'am."

"Thank you."

After several minutes, two orderlies in full hazmat gear showed up with a gurney. One of them spoke briefly with the nurse. She nodded toward Sylvia.

"Where is the patient, ma'am?" asked one of the orderlies.

"This way." Sylvia led them out to her car and opened the passenger door. She leaned inside and tried to remain matter-of-fact. "Todd, they're ready for you." She pointed to the gurney. "Just get on that and lie down."

"Are you sure this is so serious?"

She nodded. "It looks like it to me. They'll run tests of course. But if it is what I think, we can't take any chances."

The orderlies adjusted the height of the gurney and helped Todd out of the car and onto it. She wanted to cry when she saw how panicked he looked when he saw their hazmat suits. She couldn't blame him.

One of them reached into a compartment beneath the

gurney and took out an undeployed IsoStat unit. The orderlies quickly arranged the layers of plastic around Todd and inflated the IsoStat until it created a chamber around him. They nodded to Sylvia and began to push Todd toward the hospital entrance. She locked the car and followed them.

They rolled Todd down the hall and stopped next to a black plastic structure with white lettering that read *Portable Decontamination Vestibule.* Sylvia felt a twinge in her gut when she realized the yellow and black biohazard symbol applied to her husband.

They opened the outer door, revealing a space inside similar to the vestibule in her lab, but larger, to allow gurneys and other equipment to pass through to the actual hospital room. Plastic shelves along one side held disposable hazmat suits.

One of the orderlies took a suit from the shelf. "Ma'am, you'll need to put this on for your own safety." He started to unfold it and show her the openings.

She took it from him. "I know how to get into one of these, thanks." She donned the suit as quickly as she could. "All right."

The orderlies opened the second door and pushed Todd inside. She followed them and shut the door behind her. The room looked like most other hospital rooms, aside from the decontamination vestibule outside its door.

"Can't you take this thing off me now?" Todd's voice had the quality of a frightened child.

One of the orderlies spoke up. "No, sir. Current protocol is to use both the portable isolation unit and controlled access for patients suspected of contracting either ASA or MRSA-II. The double protection is necessary if either is the diagnosis—especially if it's ASA. You'll be tested, of course, to be sure. But unless and until it is ruled out ..."

The other orderly turned to her and spoke gently. "You can stay, ma'am. The doctor will be in shortly. When you do wish to leave, please remove the suit and leave it in the marked receptacle in there for proper disposal." He pointed toward the vestibule.

"Thank you." Sylvia watched them leave, then flinched when they shut the door. There was something final and damning about the sound. She turned to Todd, who lay, pale and silent, within his IsoStat. "I never thought I'd wish MRSA-II on anyone, but I really hope that's what this is. Lucracillin is incredibly effective for it."

Moments later, a doctor in full hazmat garb entered the room. Sylvia figured she'd better get used to that sight.

"Hello, I'm Dr. Williams."

Sylvia introduced herself and Todd. "I'm a research scientist at Horton Drugs. I'm familiar with the MRSA-II pathogen, and have also … heard about the ASA pathogen that has been spreading. I'm concerned my husband may have one … or the other … of those infections, given his symptoms."

"I've been dealing with both here lately. First thing I'll do is run tests to see which it is. Very important when determining the treatment."

"Yes, I know." Sylvia knew all too well. Lucracillin for one; hopes and wishes and palliative care for the other. "If you don't need me for a few minutes, I need to make a call."

"That would be fine. I'd like to do a brief exam first, then order the tests right after. If I'm not still here when you return, just be sure to put on a suit before reentering the room."

"I will, thanks." She leaned over Todd. "I'll be back in just a few minutes, okay?"

Todd nodded, his lips a thin line.

Sylvia entered the vestibule, then removed and disposed of her suit. She left in search of a private place where she could make her call. She walked down the hall, eventually finding the visitors' lounge. It was deserted, at least for the time being. So she stepped inside and called Jerry on her PortiComm to tell him what had happened.

"Well, I hope the tests prove you wrong."

"Thanks, but I don't think that's likely. Todd was perfectly fine this morning, and you should see him now. MRSA-II doesn't move that fast. And his skin. The tissue death is already substantial." She fought off tears. "I wish to God I was wrong."

"What are you going to do?"

"The doctor's in there with him now. They're going to run tests to verify what he has before they decide on treatment.

Jerry, I'm sorry, I know we both need to be working on this, but I need to be here for now."

"I understand. I'll keep at it on my end, and I'll update Phil for you. Do what you need to do."

"Thanks, Jerry. I really appreciate it. I'm just so … scared that he has it. Oh, God." She swallowed hard and tried to calm herself with a deep breath. But she'd learned too much about the mutant form of her pathogen not to be terrified.

"Sylvia?"

She wiped a tear from her cheek. "Yeah?"

"Take good care of yourself. You've been exposed now."

"I know. I used a lot of rubbing alcohol to try to minimize the contamination, but I don't know how effective that will be. I just have to hope I didn't pick it up. God, Jerry, he was at the law school teaching today. I don't even want to think of how many of his students might have been exposed—and who they've exposed since."

"I wonder if we should try again with Phil on the quarantine question. Maybe he'll listen now."

"I don't know anymore. How would anyone know *who* to quarantine? And would it be in time? Like the students. We don't yet have confirmation Todd has ASA, and we don't know which students got close enough to him, and all that. I wonder if the better thing would be some more general order for people to stay home from work, school, everything until a cure is found."

"That might be easier to swallow than forced medical quarantine. Quite a few people are self-selecting to do that as it is. But … to *require* everyone to stay home from school and work and everything until a cure is found. I don't know about that."

"Every way I think about this leads to a brick wall of some sort. I can't even think straight right now."

"I'm sorry. You go be with Todd. I'll take care of things on this end, okay? Take care of yourself, Sylvia."

"Yeah, I'll try." Sylvia headed back to Todd's room, and found Dr. Williams emerging from the outer door of the vestibule. He no longer wore the hazmat suit, but he did wear a worried look. He glanced at her as she approached.

"I'm sorry." He shook his head. "It's not MRSA-II."

CHAPTER 50

Sylvia awoke, a bright glare piercing her eyelids. Turning away from the light, she opened her eyes and found herself crumpled in an unfamiliar plastic chair. Then she remembered where she was and why. She checked the time. Just after 8:30 in the morning. She pushed her hair out of her eyes, mindless of her appearance.

She pushed herself out of the chair, stretched briefly to work out the worst of the kinks, then headed for Todd's hospital room. Given the gravity of his condition, the hospital staff had given her permission to ignore the posted visiting hours—as long as she suited up before entering his room.

The biohazard sign hadn't lost its chilling effect on her. She averted her eyes and entered the vestibule to don her hazmat gear. She adjusted the face mask, then took a deep breath to brace herself. Fearful of what she would find, she forced herself to open the inner door and enter Todd's room.

She stepped over to his bed and gazed at him as he lay enclosed within the IsoStat. He looked no better than he had last night. In fact, he looked markedly worse, despite the IV fluids and supportive medications he'd received through the night. His closed eyes lay in dark, sunken pits in his chalk-white face. His breath came in shallow fits and starts. He didn't even realize she was there. She hoped that was from the sedation.

But worst of all was the necrosis that ate his flesh. The patch that had started out as merely itchy skin had spread at a frightening pace—down his arms, onto his trunk, and onto his legs. Hospital staff had tried to keep up with it by dressing and re-dressing it as it spread, but they'd already fallen behind.

Lesions extended out from beneath the blood-and-serum-soaked bandages.

And where the necrosis had spread, the resulting tissue destruction exposed muscle and bone.

Trembling with guilt and fear, Sylvia gazed down upon what she had helped create. She had a textbook idea of what the pathogen did to its victims from the Pathosym models, and now she was being treated to a firsthand view of it. On her own husband. She had to do something, but what?

She decided not to wake him. Not right now. She hurried quietly from the room, stripped out of the hazmat suit, and returned to the visitors' lounge to call Jerry.

She gave him a quick update on Todd's condition, then asked what progress he had made.

"I wish I had something to report, but I don't. Still hitting the same brick wall. I promise you, I'm running the tests as fast as the Pathosym can process them. Just not getting a line on the pathogen's vulnerability yet."

Sylvia sat down in one of the hard plastic chairs, her legs suddenly weak. "Something *has* to work, it just *has* to."

"I told you, truly, I'm working on this as fast as possible. I don't know what else to do. I'm sorry, I—"

"Todd's going to *die* unless something is done. You didn't see him. You can't possibly appreciate how vicious this thing is until you see it with your own eyes. Talk to Phil. Try to come up with something, even if it's not fully tested. Anything. Please!"

She ended the call, put her face in her hands, and cried. She knew Jerry was telling the truth and was surely working as fast as he could, but it wasn't good enough. It just wasn't good enough.

CHAPTER 51

Phil Horton sat at his desk, checking the latest news on his FloaTouch display. He jabbed at the icon to switch it off. He was sick to death of the whole damned thing. And now Sylvia's husband had contracted the damned ASA mutation to boot. Oh, how he wished he could just disappear, leave all this behind as if it never happened. Too late to wish that now.

A soft beep from his PortiComm signaled an incoming call from Jerry. Anxious for some good news, he answered.

"What's happening? Any progress?"

"No, sorry. I'm working the Pathosym to the max, but still have no progress to report. I'm calling for Sylvia. She just updated me on Todd's condition. It's not looking good. Sounds like the necrosis is progressing quickly."

Phil put a hand to his forehead. "I'm really sorry to hear it. She must be in rough shape, having to watch that. And knowing she was exposed in the process."

"Yeah, she's sounding pretty desperate, as you can imagine. She asked me to see if there was anything they could try for him, even something not fully tested. I've got absolutely nothing right now. I, uh, know this is a tricky thing to ask, but I was wondering if you could check with Denali and see if they're working on this, too. At this point, maybe we should even work together on something with them. I don't know what else to do."

Phil realized he hadn't told Jerry and Sylvia that Horton was in competition with Denali again. He'd thought they were under enough pressure to find the cure without burdening them with that. He thought for a moment. The death toll was only going to rise. And now ASA had struck close to home. Given the widespread outbreak, he could probably still conceal Horton's role in the creation of this disaster. Maybe they *should* work together instead of in competition, given the stakes.

"All right, I'll call Tremaine and see what they have going. I think you're right. We've no other choice, given these developments."

"Thanks. I'll let Sylvia know."

Phil ended the call and took a deep breath. He gritted his teeth and made the call.

CHAPTER 52

Dan Tremaine felt a sudden urge to party as he ended the call. Despite Horton Drugs' recent dead cat bounce on the stock market, Denali Labs was still soundly kicking the ass of all of BigPharma by every measure—even with the markets in turmoil from the ASA epidemic. Profits were at an all-time high, as was Denali's stock price.

So it was delicious frosting on the cake to have Phil Horton call today, begging for help. His desperation also meant that Denali would undoubtedly produce the winning drug first and snag yet another lucrative federal government contract for the manufacture and distribution. He laughed as he pondered what Denali would be able to do with so much profit. Such a good problem to have.

Dan called Vince to check on his progress.

"We're nearly ready. Late yesterday, the simulations closed in on a new compound. It looks good in the model, but I need to expose a colony to the drug to verify the sensitivity."

"How quickly will you be able to test it on a colony?"

"I have it all teed up, ready to start. Should have the results in a few hours. The delay is in waiting for the colony to replicate sufficiently first, rather than the Pathosym's computing speed."

"Hm. Well, we have a situation that I think calls for a parallel testing path. I just got a call from Phil Horton. Not only are they making zero progress on their testing, but the husband of one of their scientists has contracted ASA. He's not expected to hold on much longer, and they wanted to know if we had anything to try, even if it isn't fully tested. They're that desperate."

Vince let out a low whistle. "I don't envy the poor fuck.

ASA's the most vicious pathogen I've ever come across."

"Do you have enough information from the modeling to determine a dosage?"

"Yes, it projected the dosage and regimen already."

"Can you prepare enough for one patient and get it shipped out ASAP while you're running the sensitivity test with the colony? They are prepared to accept the risks. They have no other viable choice and they know it."

"Sure can. I'll get right on it."

"Thanks. I'll let them know it's coming."

"Thanks, Dan. I really appreciate it."

Phil then called Jerry with the news.

"I'd call Sylvia myself, but she's probably with Todd and I didn't want to leave all this on a voice mail. Let her know next time she checks in with you. The drug has been tested for efficacy, potential side effects, and dosage through Pathosym modeling, but they haven't yet tested on a live culture of the pathogen. So, it looks good, but the final test isn't in yet. Given Todd's condition, it seems a reasonable risk to take."

"I agree. When will it be here?"

"I'm hoping within the day. They have to package up enough for a complete treatment regimen, and then I understand they're going to air courier it here on a Denali private plane."

"Great. I hope it's soon enough, though. Last time I heard from Sylvia, Todd had lost a tremendous amount of tissue. The necrosis and skin destruction has spread to most of his body, and it's eating into fascia and muscle in some parts. His GI tract is showing definite signs of compromise, too. It won't be long—"

Phil ran a shaky hand through his hair. "I know. I can't imagine a more devastating superbug … and I don't want to. How is Sylvia holding up?"

"About as you'd expect. I don't think she's slept or gone home since he was admitted."

"Is she … *well*? At least so far? She was exposed, and she's under terrific stress now."

"So far, she hasn't mentioned any symptoms. I'm hoping

she managed to avoid enough direct contamination to keep from contracting it herself."

"Well, hopefully that holds."

"Phil, I'm really worried about her. Not just because she could contract it, but she's blaming herself for the entire epidemic. She absolutely blames herself for Todd's condition. I don't know what she will do if he—"

"I should never have asked you both to develop the damned thing. Never. I shouldn't have egged her on to introduce it to the population when you objected. If anyone's to blame, it's me."

After a pause, Jerry continued. "Well, there isn't much use in recriminations now. Won't change anything. The best we can hope for is that Denali's drug does the job. That would be good news for Todd and Sylvia—and for everyone. My God, if they've found the cure, we'll finally have a weapon for this thing and can start to fight it. This just *has* to work."

"Yeah. Well, let her know it's coming. Thanks."

Phil ended the call and put his face in his hands.

Jerry was right. It just *had* to work. The epidemic had to be stopped, and fast.

Even if it meant it would cement Denali's dominance of the BigPharma landscape for years to come.

CHAPTER 53

Clad in her hazmat gear, Sylvia sat in a chair next to Todd's bed, cradling the precious package in her lap. The experimental drug from Denali Labs had just arrived at the hospital with instructions to deliver it to her personally. She'd had an alert put out for Dr. Williams to let him know it had arrived and was ready to be administered.

She gazed over at Todd, sleeping the sleep of the drugged in his IsoStat. Dr. Williams had decided to place him in an induced coma. He feared the extensive internal and external tissue destruction would create such intense pain that the shock of it would kill Todd. If the pathogen didn't kill him first.

He barely looked human as he lay there, covered in seeping bandages. The disease was progressing so quickly that it was impossible to keep the dressings clean and fresh for long. To make up for the constant loss of fluid, saline IVs and bottles of blood substitute were kept flowing into veins in the less damaged portions of Todd's arms and legs.

She looked down at the package in her lap. Would it save him? So much harm had already been done that his systems were on the verge of collapse. But she had to hope. The Pathosym models were usually spot-on. She'd never encountered an instance where the live colony test didn't confirm the models; it was just something that was routinely done before shipping a new drug application off to the FDA. The extra precaution was a holdover from the old days of live human and animal testing.

Moments later, Dr. Williams rushed into the room in his hazmat suit. "Let's see that. I presume they included the dosage instructions?"

"They said they would. I haven't opened it yet."

"All right." He unsealed the box and reviewed the slip of instructions included inside. He nodded to himself, then took a fresh syringe from the cabinet beside the bed. He tore off the wrapper, drew a dose from the vial, and injected it into a port in one of the IV tubes.

"There. It calls for an IV dose every eight hours. I'll make sure that order is in, and I guess now we wait to see what happens. In a few hours, I'll test the level of ASA in his blood to see if the drug is having an effect. With tissue destruction this extensive, it may be impossible to determine progress just by observation."

Sylvia nodded. "Makes sense. Thanks."

Dr. Williams left the room to attend to other patients. Sylvia just sat in her chair, staring at Todd—and willing the drug to take effect and save him.

CHAPTER 54

Exhaustion lay like a heavy weight on Sylvia's aching shoulders as she slumped in her chair. She yawned inside her stuffy hazmat suit. The hours since Dr. Williams had administered the first dose to Todd had passed ever so slowly. They'd taken a blood sample a while ago, and she didn't know whether to be hopeful or not. Todd didn't look one bit different to her.

Dr. Williams entered the room. "Good afternoon, Sylvia."

She couldn't read his face well enough through the hazmat mask to see if he had good or bad news for her. She straightened herself in her chair and tried to prepare herself for news of either kind.

He stepped over to Todd's bedside and peered through the IsoStat at him from head to toe as if inventorying the tissue damage. Then he fussed with the IV flows longer than seemed necessary before turning to face her.

Sylvia remained frozen in her chair. She didn't trust her legs to support her right now if she tried to stand. "What is it? What did the test say?"

"Sylvia, there are two things going on here. The test results came back, and it looks like the drug is effective. The blood level of ASA is markedly reduced with just the one dose. And what specimens are still present appear weak, lethargic. They're not multiplying. So in that respect—"

"Oh my God! That's great news—" Sylvia fought off tears of relief.

Dr. Williams held up a hand. "But there's more to it than that. The drug appears to have arrested the infection, and looks like it will eradicate it—given enough time. His tissue damage appears to have stopped progressing, too. But … the damage is already so extensive that I'm afraid even with the drug, he may not survive."

Sylvia suddenly felt dizzy and had to lower her head to avoid passing out. She held up a hand. "Just a minute. Give me a minute." A strange wave of heat passed through her, making her uncomfortably hot inside her hazmat suit. She wanted to just tear it off, to run from the room screaming. It couldn't be true. They got the drug, they've come this close to curing Todd, but *it was too late*?

After a few minutes, the dizziness passed and she carefully sat up, sweat forming on her hairline. "Are you … sure? I mean, if the drug stops the infection, then can't his body focus purely on healing?"

"In theory, yes. But here, the damage was incredibly extensive already. The necrosis spread over 90% of his body in just twenty-four hours. And it's not just on the surface. There are several lesions where the muscle has been destroyed, leaving exposed bone. That means entire swathes of blood vessels, nerves and lymphatic pathways have been destroyed as well. And his GI tract … there is evidence of internal bleeding, probably from internal necrosis. I don't dare bring him out of the induced coma for the pain he would likely experience."

"Oh." Sylvia heard the doctor's words but fought hard against accepting them.

"What are you doing?"

"Huh?"

"Don't you realize you're scratching your arm?"

"No, I didn't." Sylvia looked down, and noticed, as if her limbs were acting on their own volition, that she was scratching her left forearm with her right hand. She hadn't even realized it itched until now.

"How do you feel?"

"What? I'm—" With mounting terror, she realized she felt weak and feverish. The shock of Dr. Williams' prognosis for Todd must have distracted her. She cast a panicked glance at the doctor.

"Take off the hazmat suit. Let's see what you were scratching."

Sylvia folded her arms protectively, as if that would stop

this all from happening. "No. No, it can't be!"

"Come on."

Reluctantly, she stood, her knees trembling, whether from fear or disease, she couldn't tell. Dr. Williams helped her out of the suit, tossed it aside, and then took her temperature with the digital gauge.

"One hundred three. Roll up the sleeve on your left arm, please."

She complied, feeling as if she had just landed in a strange and terrible dream. She glanced down and gasped when she saw the lesion. Just like Todd's, only smaller.

For now.

"Roll up the other sleeve. I need to take a blood sample for immediate testing."

She collapsed into the chair and did as she was told, so upset she didn't even feel the needle.

"I'm going to get this to the lab right away, but I think I know what it's going to say. You have a decision to make."

"What?"

Dr. Williams squatted down and looked straight into her eyes. "If you've contracted ASA, there is only one apparent cure—the sample drug they sent for Todd. We know it's effective in arresting the pathogen. But there is only enough left for one person, and any delay in administering it could be ... fatal."

Sylvia stared at him. This was all happening way too fast. She hadn't even processed Todd's prognosis and now Dr. Williams was thinking she had it, too?

"Sylvia. If you have ASA, you must start on the Denali drug right away. You'll have to use the supply that was meant for Todd. We don't have enough for both of you—and we don't have time to ask for more." He took her by the shoulders. "I can't save both of you. Do you understand what I'm saying?"

She shook her head and waved him off. "I can't ... think right now."

He stood. "All right. I'll get the test running and we'll talk when the results come in. Should only take fifteen or so minutes. I'll be back."

Alone with Todd, the room silent except for the soft tones

of the various monitors, Sylvia curled into a semi-fetal position in her chair and tried to absorb what had just happened. Out of the corner of her eye, she spotted the lesion on her left arm and, repulsed, held it away from her and turned her head in the other direction.

Dr. Williams' words began to sink in. If the test was positive, she had to choose between her life and Todd's. Well, maybe not. Even with the drug, Dr. Williams didn't seem to think he'd make it. She almost didn't care about herself right now. It was her fault Todd was in the condition he was. She deserved to get the disease.

She gazed over at Todd again, Dr. Williams' words echoing in her head. He didn't dare bring him out of the induced coma because of the pain he would surely experience. She wanted so badly to talk to him, to tell him she was sorry, so sorry. To let him have his say in what decisions were made.

But she likely would never again be able to talk to Todd. Ever. Suddenly she felt like she'd already lost him. She rested her head on the chair arm and sobbed.

A short while later, Dr. Williams returned. He cleared his throat.

She looked up, her vision blurred with tears. "What?"

"It's confirmed. You've contracted ASA. I understand you don't want to deal with this right now. I really do. But time is of the essence. If you're going to take the drug, you need to start right now, and we need to conserve the rest of the supply for you."

She looked over at Todd. "How sure are you that he won't pull through if he finished the regimen?"

"I can't be 100% sure, but in my professional opinion, his condition has gone way too far, even though the drug appears to be highly effective." He shook his head. "You, on the other hand, are very early in the process, and may have an excellent chance of a full recovery."

She hung her head. "All right, then. I'll take the drug." She looked up at the doctor. "But please, keep doing all you can for Todd, just in case."

"We will. We'll continue with palliative care, and see what we can do to try to encourage healing, now that the damage has at least been arrested. I'm concerned about not running the complete drug regimen on him, that we didn't fully eradicate the pathogen, but again, there is just no choice here. I don't dare short you more than the one dose he's already had. If Denali can produce some more of the drug quickly, we can put him back on it. But you need to come first." He took a syringe from the cabinet and filled it with a dose from the vial. "Give me your right arm, Sylvia."

She extended her arm and gazed at Todd as Dr. Williams injected the lifesaving drug into her vein.

"I'm sorry, Todd."

VICTORY

CHAPTER 55

"I don't usually do this in the office—well, not *too* often, anyway—but I think it's called for today, don't you?" Dan Tremaine stood at his desk and prepared to pop the cork on a cold bottle of Krug Grande Cuvee.

Vince Calhoun had to smile. Somehow, he didn't think Dan had too much trouble finding reasons to party when he felt the urge. But this time he had to agree. Today was a very auspicious day for the company—*and* for their respective bank accounts.

"I'd say so. The FDA approved our Hercacillin as the sole drug effective against ASA, and the federal government was all too happy to take over manufacturing and distribution given the scope of the epidemic. And all of it in record time."

"Yeah, the ASA pathogen couldn't have behaved more to our specifications than if we'd designed it ourselves. That's some superbug." Dan poured them each a glass of the champagne and handed one to Vince.

"This one damned near brought down the economy—especially with the travel restrictions that were put in place. Even with Hercacillin's efficacy, we came way too close to the point where even the fastest manufacturing and distribution would have been too late to stop a worldwide pandemic." Vince paused and sipped some of his champagne. "This one really scared me—even more than MRSA-II."

"This *was* uncomfortably close, even for my taste. If we'd designed this one and had control of the schedule, I'd have pushed things about as far as we did with MRSA-II, and then brought out the drug. That worked out fine, with a smaller body count."

"I'm glad to see you wouldn't have taken it this far if you'd had the choice. I've started working on the next superbug, and wanted to be sure where you stood on that point."

"That reminds me. With all the profit we're already pulling in on Hercacillin—not to mention Lucracillin—I want you to know you'll be seeing a sizeable bonus in your next check." He raised his glass. "You really earned it. Sounds like this one was a tough one to pin down, even with your modified Pathosym." He gulped the rest of his champagne and poured himself another glass. "Horton didn't stand a chance to crack this in time, not with their old-school Pathosym."

"Thanks, Dan. I'll have to think of something fun to spend it on." He sipped his champagne. "You know, that whole business with Horton struck me as odd. He was in direct competition with us on this. He essentially conceded the race when he called you for help."

"He was worried about his scientist's husband. And she was exposed as well. So he had a staff member with a personal stake. He probably couldn't ignore that, or thought he couldn't."

"Well, I still have a funny feeling about how that all went down. Do you think they might have engineered ASA?"

Dan thought for a minute. "Well, if they did, they were pretty stupid to release it without having a companion drug ready." He smiled and took another sip. "I think it's clear to everyone—if it wasn't already—that Horton is a second-rate, has-been pharma company. They were on the way down when Denali came on the scene, and we've been eating their lunch consistently ever since."

"Maybe they thought they figured out our business model and tried to copy it and leapfrog us. If so, it sure went horribly wrong for them. And for a lot of victims." Vince shook his head. "I really do wish that many people didn't have to die before this was contained. If they did engineer ASA, they sure engineered the most deadly and dangerous superbug ever."

"That it was. Hopefully, they don't try that again. Leave it to the experts, right?"

"Right!"

Dan raised his glass and clicked it with Vince's in a toast.

Then he reached into his upper right desk drawer. "How about a little Stardust, Vince?"

He held up his hand. "Oh, no. I only make that up for you. I haven't ever tried it myself."

Dan busied himself with arranging a few lines on the small mirror. "Well, it's great stuff. You should try it just this once. To celebrate."

Vince hesitated. He'd designed the drug at Dan's request, and so he well knew its physiological effects from computer modeling. Like cocaine, but with all of the good and none of the bad. But he hadn't tried it himself because he feared he'd enjoy it a little too much and might end up a regular user like Dan. But maybe just once ...

"All right, I'll try it." He took one of the disposable straws and inhaled a line. He sat down and followed Dan's example of inhaling deeply and putting his head back as the effects kicked in. First, he felt a comfortable, glowing warmth all over, head to toe. That was from the drug's stimulative effects on the cardiovascular system, as he expected. But then, something else happened. He began to feel godlike, as if there was nothing he couldn't do—a feeling beyond anything he'd ever experienced.

Vince smiled. This must be what it felt like to be Dan Tremaine. He liked how it felt.

CHAPTER 56

"You're kidding." John Humphrey's eyes widened as he absorbed the news.

"I wish I were, but I suppose it isn't that surprising on some levels." President Coleridge was used to having unfettered power, and the discovery that someone else had power over *him* did not sit well.

"Surely there's some mistake. Is the CIA absolutely sure of their intelligence on this?"

"Rock solid. They checked and rechecked. They expressed no doubt whatsoever that Denali Labs was behind the MRSA-II outbreak. Makes me wonder about the GIS and ASA outbreaks, too. I have no proof on those yet, but if they pulled off MRSA-II—and then were essentially *rewarded* for it by the federal government—I think it's safe to assume they had a hand in those outbreaks as well."

"My God. So, will the AG prosecute?"

"Hell, no."

"Why not?"

"Don't you see? Tremaine's got us by the balls. If he did what he did, do you think for an instant that he would hesitate to develop and threaten to release some other deadly pathogen to keep us from prosecuting? I have no doubt in my mind he would do that, and I can't risk the security of the Homeland."

"But what's to stop him from developing a new pathogen just to get another government contract for the drug?"

"Nothing."

"Then what are you going to do?"

"I've told the CIA to seal its files on this investigation. We won't attempt to prosecute. But … we need to make it attractive for Denali to work with us on a different level, one that we can control. One that we can actually benefit from. I don't like lying down with dogs, but sometimes it's the only thing to do."

John leaned forward in his chair. "What are you thinking, sir?"

"I'm going to have a frank discussion with him about what we know, and then ask him to partner—confidentially, of course—on developing a pathogen we can use proactively to defend the Homeland, as well as the curing drug that would be distributed to necessary persons, were the need to use such a pathogen ever to arise."

"Sounds like a win-win, sir."

"Yes, it does solve a lot of problems, doesn't it?"

CHAPTER 57

Phil Horton sat behind his desk for the last time, and was glad of it. Boxes littered the floor all around his office. His desktop was bare. His work was done. His successor, Dennis McKenzie, sat in a chair opposite him. Phil thought he looked inappropriately eager, much like a vulture that had just spotted some tasty road kill, but he chose to not comment on that.

"I wish you luck, Dennis. I really do. I just can't do this anymore. BigPharma has morphed into a world I just can't and won't compete in. Now you know what was going on behind the scenes most of this past year, and I'm sure you can understand why I couldn't reveal it to anyone else until now. Denali has a business model that I would never have come up with myself, and I foolishly tried to beat them at their own game." He stared down at his desk, his eyes burning with exhaustion. "And I'll never be able to forgive myself for what happened because of it."

"But you were trying to keep Horton Drugs alive. To do that, you had to compete."

Phil raised his eyes and gazed at Dennis. "And that's just it. I don't have the stomach to compete that way. I hope you have better luck playing Tremaine's game, if that's what it takes to keep Horton on the map. I'm done."

Dennis shrugged one shoulder. "Well, there were lessons to be learned and I think we can apply them going forward and do a better job next time."

Phil tried to ignore the queasy feeling he got from Dennis and his casual attitude. "GIS is still common enough that sales of Spectracillin continue to do well. Horton Drugs had one foot in the grave last year, and now it's at least solvent and a going concern.

But it's way the hell behind Denali in revenues, profit margin, and market share. So Horton could at least survive the foreseeable future as it is. It's up to you now to decide how far to push to catch up with Denali."

Dennis leaned forward. "Oh, I intend to beat them at their own game. Tremaine thinks he's God. We'll show him. Horton will overtake Denali if it's the last thing I do."

"Well, I wish you the best." He glanced around his office. "If you don't mind, I'd like to be alone for a bit before I clear out."

Dennis stood. "Oh, sure. I understand. Take all the time you need." He shook hands with Phil, turned and left.

Phil went over and closed his office door, his hand lingering on the knob for a moment. Dennis was just the fresh blood needed to take on Denali. That much was evident. But he'd have to hire some new staff. Sylvia had never been the same since Todd died, and was still on some extended leave arrangement. He somehow doubted she would ever return. Jerry had quietly resigned and disappeared not long after Dennis' appointment had been announced. He had enough time in that he probably just planned to retire from an industry he could no longer believe in.

Phil stepped over to his window and gazed down at the Horton Drugs campus. He'd always loved it—the graceful, calm, collegiate look of it. The fall leaves had taken hold again, creating a glorious blaze of scarlets and oranges and golds. He smiled. There was nothing as beautiful as that sight; there never would be.

He opened the window and leaned out. He took a deep breath of the fresh, crisp fall air. A breeze caused the trees to dance in the late afternoon light.

It was so beautiful, but his soul felt filthy with guilt. Sick and putrid. All the deaths. All his fault. Nothing he could do to make it better, to wash it all away, to bring back all those victims.

Nothing at all.

Phil made a sudden decision. He climbed out of the window and stood, teetering, on the ledge. He took in his most cherished view one last time, to last him forever.

Then he closed his eyes and jumped.

CHAPTER 58

Sylvia reclined on her living room couch with the curtains drawn. She preferred it that way. The darkness made it harder to see all the reminders of Todd that surrounded her.

The darkness also made it harder for her to see just how much work she had ahead of her to pack it all up and move. Maybe she should just try to sell off as much as she could and give away the rest.

She knew she'd done the right thing in accepting that job offer in North Carolina. She wanted to live far away from the Horton campus, from where she'd lived with Todd—in fact, she wanted to be as far away as possible from the life she'd had up until now.

The new job was a teaching position at the university out there. She wouldn't be in the lab anymore, and she sure as hell wouldn't be designing any bacteria or drugs ever again. No more playing God. No more tinkering with nature. She would be teaching freshman-level biology, and that was good enough for her.

Phil had been generous about giving her paid time off to try to heal and figure out what she wanted to do. She owed him the courtesy of letting him know her plans.

She sat up straight, took a breath and made sure her emotions were in check, then called him on her PortiComm.

"Dennis McKenzie here."

She frowned. "Who?"

The voice at the other end sounded as perplexed as she felt. "I'm Dennis McKenzie, CEO of Horton Drugs. Who's calling?"

"Where is Phil Horton?"

"Who is this?"

"Sylvia Creston. I … work there. I've been on leave for a few months."

"Oh. You." A pause. "Haven't you heard?"

"Heard what?"

"Apparently not. About Phil. He … passed away several weeks ago. He'd just turned over the reins to me—"

"Passed away? He wasn't that old. What happened?"

"You really didn't hear? Well, he … committed suicide. Didn't leave a note. Police think he didn't plan it out, just did it. Jumped out his office window."

Sylvia gasped. All along, she'd thought Phil took the whole disaster rather casually, considering the death toll. She'd been out of touch with most everyone since going on leave, and so never did hear the news.

"Thank you. I just called to say I won't be returning to Horton Drugs." She spoke the words mechanically, as if from a script, and hung up.

REBIRTH

CHAPTER 59

Jenny Russell squinted as she watched over her kindergarten class on their play break. She pawed at her eyes and wondered if she was catching pinkeye or something. Weak morning sunlight just shouldn't hurt like that.

Her little boys and girls ran screaming around the playground with their typical boundless energy. She usually enjoyed running around with them, but today she'd been dragging ever since she got up. The annual flu bug must have decided to pay her a visit. If she felt like this tomorrow, she'd have to call in a sub so she didn't spread it and make her kids sick.

Jenny checked her watch. "Time to go back in now! Come on. We'll practice the alphabet a little before lunch, how about that?"

The kids started filing back into the classroom, chattering and jostling each other. She smiled as she watched them. Her teacher friends envied the rapport she had with her kids. She didn't think she did anything special, she just got along well with them.

Once back inside, her kids took their seats and squirmed in anticipation of the next activity. She stepped to the front of the room, then leaned against the whiteboard a moment. The number of kids doubled and swam for a moment in her vision.

"What's the matter, Ms. Russell? You don't look so good." Jeffie Lawson, the de facto leader of the class, gazed at her from the front row with concern in his large blue eyes. The other kids whispered to each other and stared at her.

"I'm okay, Jeffie. I just need to sit down a minute." She hurried the few steps to her desk and sat, never so grateful in her life for a chair.

"Eeew!"

"Gross!"

Jennie looked up to see universal disgust registered on all the kids' faces. She rubbed at a tickle on her upper lip, then realized it was wet with blood. She covered her face with one hand and reached for a tissue with the other.

"It's okay, just a little nosebleed. I'll be all right in a minute."

It swam in warm, thick, comforting blood. It swam with others of its kind, in the darkness.

It had no concept of night and day, nor of the passage of time. It just *was*.

Sudden bright light intruded. It felt chilled, exposed.

It felt *threatened*.

A sudden desperate survival instinct took over as it quickly sought out another of its kind. The two entwined, becoming one single organism, exchanging essential genetic material, interweaving it in various combinations until the merged organism felt comfortable with its new surroundings. Then the single, modified organism cleaved into two.

And each began to multiply. Each knew the importance of establishing a new colony that could not only survive, but could also defend itself, in the new environment.

The colony prepared itself for a new battle. A battle it intended to win, because evolution only rewards the fittest.

Jennie checked her watch. Only a couple of hours left in the school day. Surely she could make it that long. Otherwise, she'd have to get someone to sub in or have the school office call all the parents to pick up their kids early. Just wasn't worth all that for a couple more hours. She glanced around the room. All the kids lay on their little pads on the floor, having their early afternoon naps. At least she could get off her feet for a little bit while they were quiet and didn't need her full attention.

She slumped in her chair. Whatever she had didn't feel quite like the flu, but it must be. Maybe there was some crazy new strain going around. She felt hot and achy, and already had that nosebleed, as well as several more bouts of dizziness she'd tried to hide from the kids.

Now it was getting harder to breathe, like she couldn't get a full breath into her lungs. Panic made her heart race and pound as she felt her throat tighten. Less and less air got in with each breath. She didn't want to scare the kids, but she needed help.

Jennie opened her mouth to scream. And nothing came out. She clutched at her throat and fought for air. She stood, knocked her chair backward, and staggered toward the door. Her knees buckled as darkness closed in.

A loud thump woke Jeffie from his nap. He sat up and saw Ms. Russell lying facedown on the floor at the front of the room. The other kids woke up and stared openmouthed at the sight.

Jeffie jumped up and ran to Ms. Russell. Something was wrong with his favorite teacher! He leaned over her motionless body.

"Ms. Russell? Ms. Russell? Wake up!" He reached over and gently shook her shoulder. Nothing happened.

The other kids crowded around, confused and scared. Jeffie didn't know what else to do. He got down on his knees, placed his cheek against the floor so he could see her face.

Jeffie screamed when he saw the blood dripping from her nose, over her blue lips, and onto the carpet..

ABOUT THE AUTHOR

Lisa von Biela worked in Information Technology for 25 years, then dropped out to attend the University of Minnesota Law School, graduating magna cum laude in 2009. She now practices law in Seattle, Washington.

Lisa began writing short, dark fiction just after the turn of the century. Her first publication appeared in *The Edge* in 2002. She went on to publish a number of short works in various small-press venues, including *Gothic.net, Twilight Times, Dark Animus, AfterburnSF,* and more. She is the author of the novels *The Genesis Code, The Janus Legacy, Blockbuster, Broken Chain, Incidental Findings,* and *Down the Brink,* as well as the novellas *Ash and Bone, Skinshift,* and *Moon Over Ruin.*

Curious about other Crossroad Press books?
Stop by our site:
http://store.crossroadpress.com
We offer quality writing
in digital, audio, and print formats.

Enter the code FIRSTBOOK
to get 20% off your first order from our store!
Stop by today!